I0586699

Sparkles and Blood

and other stories

Copyright Alex McGilvery 2015

Second Edition

ISBN 978-0-9959926-5-8

Celticfrog Publishing

Table of Contents

Frost and Stone

Frost and Stone

Chapter One

Siobhan screamed until she thought her throat would tear. If she screamed loud enough she could drown out the voices of her parents telling her how she shamed them, again.

"You should know better, Siobhan O'Hullan," her mother said as if Siobhan sat doe eyed and attentive. "We've told you again and again that you must be respectful at school. Your father has a position in the community."

"Mr. Riordan phoned me," her father said, "he's a deacon at the church. They are already concerned about you."

"They didn't hire me, did they?" Siobhan said. "No one asked me if I wanted to live in this piss-ant town. Your precious Mr. Riordan spends his day peering down my shirt and hoping for a glimpse."

"You need to dress modestly," her mother said. "It's the work of the devil, these girls parading about in next to nothing."

"We wear a school uniform, Mom. Short skirts and thin white blouses so the teachers can get their jollies. I'd wear my parka all day if we were allowed. All I did was ask him to back off and stop drooling all over me."

"You told him to, 'effing keep his creepy effing eyes to himself'. In front of the whole school no less."

"I heard he mauled at one of the girls, and got her knocked up too."

"She was a wicked girl and a liar. It was one of those boys that she tempted into sin," her mother said.

"We'll never know since she went off and hung herself."

"That just proves that she was an evil girl. No good girl would think of such a thing." Siobhan caught her father wincing a little, but he didn't speak up. He never did. Her mother would have most of the world in hell and not think twice about it.

"That's your answer for everything isn't it?" Siobhan said. "People are evil, sinful, worthy only of burning in hell. Well let me tell you, the worst people are the ones who sit in the front of your church and pretend to be good."

"We are all sinners," her father said.

"Not all of us rape girls and kill them to cover it up!" Siobhan knew she'd gone too far when her mother's face went white. She fled out into the damp of the November weather. Her anger kept her warm for the first half block, then she started shivering in her thin sweater.

"What good are parents when they won't listen?" she asked the grey sky. "Why don't you tell them, hey? They might listen to you. Come down here and let them know that the deacons who run their church are hypocrites. Just one bolt of lightning, just one!"

"I bet I know who you'd want it to be aimed at," Pwyll stepped out from where he'd been leaning against a tree and wrapped his jacket around her shoulders.

"You were waiting for me?" Siobhan let his warmth sink into her. Pwyll pulled a second coat out from behind the tree and took her hand.

"I heard you while I was doing my paper route," he said. "I went and got an extra coat and waited. You always walk this way when you're angry." He took her hand and a different warmth ran up her arm.

"You be careful, or my mother will have you burning in hell."

"I'm Catholic," Pwyll said, "I'm already headed for the flames."

Siobhan sighed. This church her dad worked in was very good at deciding who were the sinners destined to burn. It hadn't always been that way. The place they were in before they came to New Franklin had been filled with laughter and fun. Everyone had been her friend. The New Franklin Chapel of God had stolen the joy from her father. Now she seemed to be trapped in the role of the devil child. She'd heard there had been a suggestion that they perform an exorcism on her.

They walked aimlessly through the streets until it started to snow. Pwyll guided them directly to her front door. He was careful to let go of her hand before they rounded the corner to her street.

"I can never figure out how you do that," she said, "I'd be lost forever."

"I don't know," Pwyll said, "I just know where I'm going."

"And that's not to Hell," Siobhan said.

Pwyll shrugged. She gave him his jacket back before he waved and walked away.

"I don't want you hanging around with that boy," her mother said from behind her. "He's foreign and Catholic."

"He's Welsh, Ma," Siobhan said, "His name is Paul, only spelled the Welsh way."

"Like English isn't good enough for him?" She held the door wide. "Upstairs and to your room. You pray for forgiveness for your rudeness to Mr. Riordan. Some prayer and fasting will do you good."

Siobhan looked at her father, but he didn't say anything. So, she climbed the stairs to her room in this house that wasn't theirs. She stared at the room and sighed. If God really answered prayers, than she would wake up one morning and find that her room was no longer pink and white. It made her feel like she was trapped inside a wedding cake. It must be because she was such a wicked girl that her life was so horrible. That was the only explanation. Everyone at the Chapel thought so and told her too.

She knelt on the thin chair pad with her back to the door. She'd told her volleyball coach that she'd hurt her knees playing soccer last summer, but the truth was she spent so much time kneeling that her legs ached all the time. The ball in her stomach was hunger and anger. She didn't know which was worse. At least hunger wasn't a sin. It was supposed to get her closer to God. What a joke.

She felt her mother staring at her back, but she refused to turn or speak. Her mother couldn't fault her for praying too hard.

So God, this is how it is going to be? You're supposed to be in charge and yet here I am starving, while I bet Riordan is stuffing his face. You're supposed to know what's in people's hearts. You saw how he was looking at me. Caitlin told me I was imagining things. He doesn't stare at her, and she leaves an extra button undone and wears a padded bra, as if she needs one. Why is it me that turns him on?

Siobhan felt her mother's presence behind her again much later at night, but once again she ignored her. She heard a sigh.

"Go to bed, Siobhan," her mother said. "Tomorrow, you will apologize to Mr. Riordan. You must learn to control yourself."

Siobhan stayed kneeling until she heard that sigh again and the presence faded. She had no idea how she knew when her mother or father were there. Sometimes other people too. It was like she felt a warmth on her skin. Her mother would call it evil and occult, so Siobhan never mentioned it and rarely gave it much thought.

Well, if I'm to apologize, you'll have to give me the words, she looked toward the fixture in her ceiling, *the only ones that I can think of will get me in bigger trouble.*

Siobhan woke early and grabbed a glass of milk and a granola bar for breakfast. She'd put on an extra camisole under her blouse and wore a bra from last year. It felt tight enough that it should make her less interesting to Riordan. Maybe her mother had never had to deal with men like Riordan. She'd gone to an all girl's school until she'd met Siobhan's father and got converted and married all at once. Siobhan had never seen her parents kiss or even touch. She wondered how they managed to produce a daughter.

"Eww," she said to herself, "let's not go there at this time of the day." She walked past Pwyll's house, but she could tell he was still in bed. The school was quiet. There was the sound of volleyball practice in the gym and faint honks from the direction of the band room. She headed for the chapel for a last consultation with God before facing Riordan. The chapel was a miniature of the church that her father worked at. Some patron saint of the congregation had died and left his millions to the church. They'd built the school as an outreach of the church. A Christian education in a secular world. People paid money to send their kids to the school. Siobhan got in because her father was the pastor in the church.

Maybe you could call my father to a different church, she thought at the stark cross at the front of the chapel. *Then I wouldn't have to go to school here and deal with Riordan*. She felt someone enter the chapel. It wasn't unusual for students to stop in, before exams it was standing room only. The person slid onto the bench beside her.

"You must learn submission," Mr. Riordan said. "It will be your place as a wife to submit to your husband."

She just managed to stop the snort before it became audible.

"There is much that I could teach you," he put his hand on her knee. Siobhan's stomach knotted and she started shaking. His hand moved up her leg and pulled her skirt with it. She felt his fingers burn again the skin of her thighs. She took a deep breath, but his hand moved faster than she thought possible to tangle in her hair. He twisted her face so she had to look at him. "I've always thought that red hair was a sign of the devil," he said in the same voice he used to drum facts about the Second World War into their heads. "It is alluring and dangerous all at once. Witches have red hair." His other hand poked through between the buttons of her blouse. "You will not wear extra clothing beneath your blouse," he said, still in that teacher's voice. "You mustn't hide your beauty."

He kissed her with the same pouncing motion that vampires used to tear out their victim's throats. She felt he was pulling the life from her. It wasn't at all what she'd imagined a kiss to be. This was hard edges and pain. He pulled away just a tiny way from her face. "I am the chair of deacons at the Chapel. If I say the word, your father will never work again. Don't make me say that word." He kissed her again and she felt his tongue trying to push past her teeth. She wondered what he would do if she puked in his mouth.

He pushed her away and walked out of the chapel. Siobhan scrubbed at her mouth trying to get the taste of him off her.

"Why didn't you stop him?" she said to the ceiling. The room was empty, really empty. She could feel when people were around her, but she had never in her life ever felt anything when she talked to God. Siobhan stood and walked out of the Chapel. She was done with this whole God thing.

She made it to the hall and puked on the floor. She threw up until she expected to turn inside out.

"Go home and clean up," Mr. Riordan said. "You are disgusting. Mind what I said."

Siobhan washed her face in the washroom, then tried to wash her shirt. The water only made the thin material transparent. She scrubbed at it with paper towels trying to dry the fabric off, but it didn't work. She'd have to walk past his office as good as naked. Her stomach rebelled and she puked into the sink.

"God, Siobhan, the place reeks," Caitlin stood behind her, and for a second Siobhan wanted to let the words pour out of her like vomit. She gritted her teeth and stayed quiet. "You'd better go home, you're no good like this." The other girl put a sweater around Siobhan's shoulders. "You can't walk through the halls like that, some boy will break something." She put her arm around Siobhan and guided her to her locker like Siobhan had gone blind.

"Thanks," Siobhan said. The words rasped at her throat.

"No problem," Caitlin said and left. Siobhan put on her parka and walked with shaking legs. The other students started to arrive and she had to fight upstream to get out the door. Once she was outside, the cold set her to shivering so violently it was hard to walk.

The walk home took her past a little strip mall. It was just a burger place, a gift shop and a drug store. Siobhan walked into the pharmacy and bought some black hair dye. If being a red head was the problem she would change. If she could have dyed her skin too she would have, but the hair would be a start.

The directions on the package made it look simple enough. Siobhan had the house to herself. She locked herself in the bathroom and started on her hair. Her mother never let her cut it and she didn't think that the package would cover all her hair. She braided it carefully, then used her mother's sewing scissors to hack through the braid just below her shoulders. The package said to wash her hair, so she turned on the shower and let the hot water run across her shoulders and turn her skin pink. She stepped out of the shower and dripped water on the floor as she toweled her hair dry. Her reflection was blurred and distorted as she worked the dye into her hair, then she dyed her eyebrows. She would have dyed the fine hairs on her arms if she thought it wouldn't have just left her with blotchy blacken skin. She'd wear long sleeve blouses and long skirts. Maybe she'd become Catholic and become a nun.

When enough time had passed, she rinsed the dye out. She didn't recognize herself. The black hair made her pale skin look white. She looked like a corpse. She imagined her flesh rotting and falling off. At least Riordan wouldn't like her as a corpse.

She heard the doorbell and put her robe on to answer the door.

"Package," the man said, "sign here." Siobhan signed. and he handed her a box that was heavier than it looked. He walked away again giving no sign he had seen her as anything but a signature on his clipboard. The black hair was working.

The box was addressed to her. She took it up to her room and opened it while sitting cross legged on her bed.

Dear Siobhan, I do hope you've forgiven me for sticking you with my name, but every generation of our family has had its Siobhan. I knew, in spite of your mother's inclinations that you were the one for this generation. I'm sending you a spirit stone from the village that our people came from. Guard it carefully, it is a piece of your heritage. The letter went on for pages. Siobhan had heard only the briefest stories of her aunt back in Ireland. Her mother talked about this elder Siobhan as if she were as dangerous as a bomb. She set the letter aside to take out the stone. It felt cold from being outside, but otherwise was nothing special. It was a plain black granite stone. Siobhan could have picked it up outside where granite surrounded them. She tossed it onto the dresser where it joined the rest of the clutter. Old trophies, pictures, even other rocks filled the top of the dresser. She didn't care about most of it, but it would be too much work to throw it out.

"What have you done!" her mother stood in the bedroom door and stared at Siobhan.

"I thought I'd try a new look," Siobhan said. They weren't the words she'd planned to say, but something stopped her words about a kiss and a threat.

"Are you *trying* to shame us?" her mother said. Then she saw the letter and the box on the bed. She looked at the address and her face changed. For a second Siobhan thought her mother had looked scared. Her mother scooped up the letter and box.

"Hey, those are mine!" Siobhan said. Instead of answering her mother slapped her hard across the face. She looked at the dresser and grabbed a rock. Siobhan just stared in shock as her mother ran out of the room with her letter and the rock.

Heat rose from her stomach and for an instant Siobhan thought she was going to be sick, then a scream poured out of her throat hot and powerful. She half expected the mirror on her dresser to shatter. She ran after her mother, but her mother was gone.

Siobhan slammed the door to her room, then for good measure she opened it and slammed it again. This time the antique mirror in the hall fell with a crash. She wedged the chair under the doorknob and started on her room. Siobhan had never thrown a tantrum before and there was something freeing about letting her anger rage free. All her life she'd been told anger was dangerous, she had to obey, submit, be a good girl.

The mirror made a satisfying smash as she hit it with her chair. She kept swinging at the dresser until both it and the chair were splinters. Trophies became missiles embedded in the wall. She used a piece of the mirror to slash her school uniform to shreds. When she was done, she used her blood to draw on her walls. She didn't know what she was drawing, but it felt right. It felt powerful. She smashed everything she could break, broke holes in the plaster walls. The rage drove her to exhaustion, then she sat in the midst of the destruction and wept.

"Now, you can't tell me that didn't feel some good."

Siobhan gasped and looked for the source of the voice. A tiny grey man sat in the centre of her bed. Siobhan stood up and backed against the wall.

"Who are you?" she said, "And where did you come from?"

"You called me," he said, "I always come when I'm called." He waved his hand at the demolished room. "This is a fine spell for a beginner."

"Spell?" Siobhan said. "You make me sound like a witch."

"You are a witch," the man said, "red hair and all. You can try to cover it up, but it will show through just the same. Besides," he leered at her, "you missed a bit."

Siobhan clutched at the robe and tied it tight shut.

"A lass like you should be happy to show off. You people used to dance naked under the moon."

He leered at her again, "It's a full moon tonight. I could teach you."

"I already have enough people trying to teach me," Siobhan said, "I don't need any more."

"Now is that any way to treat someone you just called to you in blood and rage?" The man on the bed started to grow bigger. "Maybe there is a first lesson I should be teaching you." When he stood up Siobhan realized he was naked. The diagrams from health class became disgustingly clear. She thought of Mr. Riordan at school.

"I wish they were dead," she said.

"Ah, now we're getting somewhere," the man said. He jumped off the bed and walked toward her. Siobhan wondered how he could manage. "What will you give me to grant your wish?"

"Are you the devil after my soul?" Siobhan felt a little foolish asking, but while she didn't feel God anywhere, this not so little man felt cold and ugly to her.

"What would I be wanting with your soul?" The grey man shook his head. "I want you."

Siobhan laughed, "Get in line, creep." The rage boiled up inside her and exploded. "You can have this," she shouted and kicked the man as hard as she could between his legs.

He fell gasping to the floor, and she thought he was having a seizure. Then she realized he was laughing.

"Done," he said and vanished.

Cold emptiness replaced the anger. How had she managed to have enough energy to do all that destruction? She dropped the robe to the floor and picked some clothes from the mess. She shook twinkling shards of mirror off them and dressed in layer after layer. It didn't matter, she was still cold. It was like ice had invaded her.

Her parents were going to kill her, really truly kill her, and then her mother would tell everyone how she was going to hell.

Siobhan thought a little flaming lake wouldn't be a bad thing right now. She picked her way out of the room and ran out of the house. She had no idea where she was going to go. She put her hands in her pocket and found a stone. She pulled it out and saw that it was the one that her aunt had sent her. Her mother must have grabbed the wrong one.

The stone was the reason for all this, but when she held it she didn't feel as cold. She put it and her hand back into her pockets and headed toward the school. She had an unfinished conversation with Mr. Riordan.

The weather forecast had predicted rain, but it started to snow. The snow suited her mood. The stone was keeping her warm now. She imagined what she was going to say to Riordan.

She walked up the stone walk to the main doors. She usually entered through the back, but the stone told her to use these doors that opened into the main foyer and the offices.

The warmth and moisture of the school air hit her face as she walked into the school. 'Academy of God's Word' declared the crest set in the tiled floor. *What did this ostentation have to do with God?* She stopped, confused in the foyer. What was she doing here? She wasn't in uniform; she was going to be so dead.

The bell rang. Students poured out of the classrooms and milled through the hall. The foyer wasn't a shortcut anywhere, so Siobhan watched the bodies bump and flow. For a second she caught a glimpse of something beneath the movement of students, some kind of order.

Then Mr. Riordan stepped out of the flow and the order vanished.

"What are you doing here?" he said, "I thought I sent you home."

Siobhan lost her words. She stared at this man who had touched her in the Chapel and couldn't think what to say. She clenched her hand on the rock. Maybe she should just hit him with the rock and leave. A flash of cold traveled up her arm like someone had shoved an icicle beneath her skin.

"I didn't get the chance to finish our discussion," her mouth said to Mr. Riordan. "You were telling me how fascinating you found red heads. I didn't feel like being part of your fascination considering what happened to the last girl who fascinated you. I'll bet you were disappointed that she wasn't a *real* redhead." Her mouth smiled at Mr. Riordan in a shape that Siobhan had never felt before. It made her powerful and dangerous. "Do you like my new look?" She swung her hair at him and caught glimpses of hair that was the black of a felt marker at the edges of her vision. Her face took on a different shape. "Someone told me I missed a spot," she said, barely above a whisper. "Do you want to see?"

Riordan tried to speak, but no words came out. Siobhan looked into his eyes and watched him lick his lips. Oh yeah, he wanted to see.

"My office," he said. It sounded to Siobhan that he had to force the words out. The students were whispering amongst themselves.

"Oh," she said, "it looks like I'm going to get a *private* session." She tossed her hair again and that strange and dangerous smile returned to her face. She led Mr. Riordan to his office. As soon as the door closed he was on her, kissing her with the same sharp edged fervour he'd shown in the Chapel. His hands were struggling to get past all the layers of clothes that Siobhan wore.

"So, that's why you make us wear skirts," her mouth said into his kisses. She thought of the naked little man and laughed. "I wonder if you will look as ridiculous." Riordan back handed her across the face. Her skin split apart under his ring and she lifted her hand from her pocket to touch her face. Somehow the rock stayed in her hand. She felt a piercing cold in her face.

"You asshole," she said. Mr. Riordan snarled and swung at her again. She blocked him with the rock in her hand. He screamed and tried to pull away from her, but some force held him in place. Siobhan's arm grew warm, then hot. She wondered why she didn't burst into flames as the heat settled into her core. She'd never felt so good in her life. There was the same giddiness when Caitlin had dared her to drink a tequila shot, but hotter, richer, more glorious.

If she was feeling good, it was clear that Mr. Riordan was not. He continued to scream as if he never needed to breathe. She finally pulled her hand away from him just to shut him up. He crouched on the floor whimpering, holding his black and twisted left hand.

"Goodbye, Mr. Riordan," she said, "I'm so glad we had this opportunity to talk."

She walked out of his office and caught a glimpse of herself in the glass. Her hair curled red and fiery around her head like a halo. There was no sign of the cut on her cheek.

"Didn't you have your hair dyed black?" one of the secretaries asked.

"The school doesn't allow students to dye their hair," Siobhan said, "and red is a much more fascinating colour." She waved at the secretaries and walked into the foyer. The last of the students were being chivvied to class. It had felt much longer in his office. He must have very good soundproofing. She looked back through the glass. One of the secretaries had atrociously dyed red hair. She gave Siobhan a nervous look and went to knock on Mr. Riordan's door.

The secretary's scream was cut off by the school doors closing behind Siobhan. She didn't know why she ever bothered with this place.

The snow fell heavily, but it melted and steamed away from her hair, the glorious warmth she'd held just minutes ago was already dissipating. She wondered what other conversations she could find as she wandered into the blizzard.

Chapter Two

Pwyll answered the phone while pushing his younger brother away with one arm.

"Pappa's Pizza Place," the twerp yelled at the top of his lungs, then ran off laughing like a hyena.

"Sorry about that," Pwyll said, "Jones residence."

"I need to speak to Paul," the woman on the other end said.

"That would be me," Pwyll said, saving the lesson on Welsh pronunciation for another day, she seemed pretty upset.

"Have you seen Siobhan?" the voice said, and he recognized the voice as Siobhan's mother. "Is she there? Are you hiding her?"

"I just got home from school," Pwyll said, "I haven't had a chance to look under the bed yet."

"Don't get smart with me, kid," she said, "I know you've been out walking with her. She has to be there."

Pwyll worked on another smart ass reply. He didn't like Siobhan's mother. The only time they talked was when she was lecturing him about something.

"Please, God, she has to be there. What have I done?" Her voice went from bossy to a wail and he heard weeping at the other end of the line. Pwyll stuffed the smart ass reply back into his head.

"Look, maybe I should come over," he said. "Give me a few minutes." He went looking for his little brother.

"Pete," he said, "I have to go out. Go over to Grandpa's for a bit."

"They don't have cable-"

"Remember *that* night?" Pwyll asked and started putting on his boots. His brother looked at him and nodded.

"A friend is having a night like that."

"OK," Pete said, "I'll text you when I get there."

The punk was a nuisance, but sometimes he got it. Pwyll figured he was lucky on the whole. He put on his coat and hat. The blizzard swirled through the door as he opened it.

"Do you need me to walk you?" Pwyll asked.

"Nah, I'll go through the back," Pete said, "I'll be fine."

Pwyll shrugged and closed the door behind him. It was faster not to argue. He put his head down and followed his sense of direction to Siobhan's front door. Her mom yanked it open and pulled him in before he had a chance to knock.

"This is all my fault," she said and fell into a chair. "I should have known I couldn't escape it. Why did she have to choose my daughter to be the one for this generation?"

"I'm not following you, Mrs. O'Hullan," he closed the door and felt immediately too hot in his parka, but he didn't want to take it off in case he needed to make a quick escape. "Chosen for what?" She didn't answer, so he wandered over to the table where some papers were crumpled. He hated to see anything with writing abused, so he flattened them out without looking at the writing until he got to the top page.

Dear Siobhan, it said.

"Don't touch that!" Mrs. O'Hullan yelled from where she was sitting. She ran over and snatched the letter from the table. She looked like she was going to tear it in two.

"No!" Pwyll said. "I mean, what if she needs something in the letter?"

"What could she need from my witch sister?"

"You mean witch like Harry Potter?"

"No, I mean witch as in giving your soul to the devil!" She tried to shred the letter, but the paper refused to tear. It looked and felt like ordinary paper, but no matter what Mrs. O'Hullan did, it would not rip. She finally pushed it at Pwyll.

"You're going to hell anyway, so what does it matter?" she said. Pwyll wanted to be insulted, but her voice came from some deep pit of despair. "What do the young know of evil?" She staggered into the living room and fell on the couch weeping like his mom had *that* night. Pwyll took the letter and went back out into the storm. He was more comfortable with wind and snow than tears. At least with the storm he couldn't be expected to do more than endure.

He walked back to his house with his hands in his pockets. He kept touching the letter in his pocket. It didn't feel like magic paper. It felt like crumpled paper and yet a full grown woman couldn't tear it apart.

He unlocked the door and stepped into the house before he thought to check his phone. No message from Pete, the punk had promised. Pwyll dialed his Grandpa.

"Hey, Pete was supposed to walk over there, then message me," he said, "can you tell that- what do you mean he isn't there? He promised he'd go straight there. Sorry Grandpa, I don't mean to yell. I'll find him." He tried to ignore the beast clawing at his gut. How long had he been at Siobhan's place? How far could a punk like his brother go in that amount of time?'

"I have to go," he said, "I'll call when I find him. No don't call the police, they'll be busy. I'll take care of it."

He put everything but Pete out of his mind. He'd done this before. *That* night, when everything had gone to pieces. He'd found his way to what he'd needed to do. It didn't make sense. He should be out in the storm yelling the little twerp's name. He put that aside. Mom would be upset; it was bad when Mom was upset. He pushed that away. He would have him back before she got home. He was sure he'd cleaned out the house. He let go of that. Only Pete mattered, only Pete, then step by step he'd find the kid. And if he was still alive he'd kill him.

Pwyll pushed the door open and walked out into the storm. It was getting dark already. The streetlights were islands of light swirling snow. It was the shadows that called him. The places the light couldn't reach pulled at him. He was empty, and they wanted to fill him. Pwyll walked forward into the wind, and when he reached the corner he turned right. He didn't wonder about Siobhan's dad when he drove past, nor did he worry that he'd left the door open. Everything was in its place as long as he didn't lose concentration on the path.

The wind blew cold on his face. He wasn't sure he had a face anymore. Snow crammed into every opening in his coat. It filled his pockets and drowned the letter. He didn't think about it. It wasn't part of the path he was walking. The night had come full on and the pull of the shadows was stronger. He'd never walked the path this long before, not even *that* night. He was empty of any thought but of Pete. He came to himself when Pete hurtled into him and knocked him into a baby snow drift.

"Sorry, sorry, sorry, sorry," Pete said endlessly. Pwyll held him tight, but the path didn't let go of him yet. There was one thing yet needed.

"Siobhan," he whispered and his stillness fractured.

"You calling your girlfriend now?" Pete said. "I want to go home. I'm cold."

They were both shivering uncontrollably. Pwyll wasn't sure he could get up, never mind walk home. The distance wasn't great, but the cold was deep inside him.

"Siobhan," Pwyll whispered again forcing the sound out between chattering teeth.

"Hey, Shevon," Pete yelled at the top of his lungs, "your boyfriend wants you."

Pwyll saw a figure walking toward him. It was a flame with a core of shadow. Then he saw it was Siobhan walking through the storm as if it were a summer day with no hat holding in her hair, a parka hung open and showed layers of black clothing. Her hands were pushed into her pockets.

"Pwyll?" she said, then again "Pwyll?" as if she were traveling a long way to speak to him. "What are you doing here? Is this your brother? What time is it? Where am I?" With each question her voice grew more urgent and upset.

"It's late Siobhan, I don't know where we are, but I need your help to get home. It's so cold." Pwyll said, or tried to say through the shaking of his body. It came out as so much nonsense.

"Oh God, Pwyll, you've got hypothermia! Why didn't you wear a hat?" She pulled him to his feet and he swayed against her. Nothing worked right. How had Pete stayed so warm? She wrapped her arms around him and muttered something. It sounded like *This better work*, but it couldn't have been because the next thing she did was kiss him. It was rough at first, but he made his arms wrap around her and kissed her back as well as he could through his icy lips. Warmth travelled from his lips to the rest of his face. Geez, was he blushing over a kiss? He would have pulled away but she wouldn't let him. The warmth moved down his body into tingling fingers and frigid toes. He gave up worrying about being embarrassed and just enjoyed the kiss.

She let go and stepped back.

"I think that's enough," she said. An edge in her voice suggested that he shouldn't argue. His pants were suddenly very uncomfortable. And she was looking right at the bulge with this strange look on her face.

"Siobhan," Pwyll said, "it's not what it looks like." She lifted her eyebrow. It was a beautiful eyebrow. Why hadn't he ever noticed before? "I don't want to..."

"No?" she said and did something with her lips and her body that made him admit he did want to, right here in the snow if she'd let him. He turned away and put a handful of snow on his face and the back of his neck.

"Yeah, it's the biggest boner I've ever had," he said with his back still turned to her, "but I won't be doing anything with it until it's the right time. I don't think this is the right time. There are some guys who'd have you on that picnic table already."

"They might try," Siobhan said. For a second Pwyll thought she was going to say something else, but instead she put her hand on his shoulder. "I think I gave you a little too much."

"Too much of what?"

"Of whatever I gave you," Siobhan swayed suddenly. "Oh crap," she said. "too much for sure."

"What do I do?" Pwyll said.

"Kiss me," she said.

He didn't need a second request. He expected more heat and more energy, but this time her lips were cold, almost icy. The energy flowed out of him and his pants fit again. She pushed him away.

"That should do," she said. She looked him in the eyes and he saw some shadow move in their depths. The shadow called to him. *What have you done?*

"Let's get home," he said, "while we're both still standing. Pete," he called out, "where did you go?"

"Oh, so you're finished?" Pete crawled out from under a picnic table pulling a bedraggled dog on a string. "Can I keep him? His name's Brac."

"You named a dog Broke?" Siobhan said.

"You should talk," Pete said. "It's Brac, it's Welsh for free."

"And how would you be knowing that?" Pwyll said.

"Brac told me." Pete tugged on the string and started away out of the park.

"Pete," Pwyll said. His brother stopped and looked at him.

"Now what?"

"Home is this way," Pwyll said.

He led the way through the dark streets to the house with the door flapping open and the hallway full of snow.

"Oh great," Pwyll said, "Mom's going to kill me."

"I'll help you clean it up," Siobhan said. She grabbed a broom and pushed the snow toward the door while Pwyll used a shovel to throw it off the porch. Even Pete helped by mopping the floor clear of the last of the snow. Brac sat and watched for a bit, then went to curl up on a mat in the kitchen.

Pwyll's mother arrived just as they finished.

"Oh," she said, "this your girlfriend? Don't make a mess, condoms in my drawer." She banged through the cupboards. "Why is there never anything to drink in this house?" She tripped over the dog and cursed. "Who let this mangy cur in the house?"

"His name is Brac!" Pete said.

"Yeah," Pwyll's mom said, "who do you think is going to pay for his food?"

"I will," Pwyll said. His mother stared at him for a minute than shrugged and staggered away to fall on the bed. He could hear her snore from where he stood.

Siobhan took his hand and squeezed it.

"I'm sorry," she said.

"It isn't easy living with what she has to live with," Pwyll said. "She just about died protecting us. Now she has to live with what happened."

"What did happen?" Siobhan asked. Pwyll looked at her. Her hair still looked like it was moving on its own. Even through the layers of her black clothes, he could see the shape that haunted his dreams. He didn't have to become his dad.

"Sometimes, I can find a path through a problem," he said, "like I was able to find Pete in the storm. I empty myself and wait for the first step to appear. It isn't like I can see the whole path at once, just one step at at time. My dad was a cop, but he drank after work and would beat up on Mom. I wanted to make it stop. That was the first time I used the path. One step at a time, until I was so far along the path that there was no turning back." He looked to see where Pete curled up beside Brac on the mat. "Did you know that someone under twelve can't be charged for a crime?" He leaned over to whisper in her ear. "Not even for shooting a cop with his own gun?"

"You shot your dad?" She went rigid with shock.

"No," Pwyll said and felt his gut twist, "I gave the gun to Pete. Dad would have killed me, but Pete was just a kid. I used my brother to kill my dad." Tears burned his eyes. Siobhan looked at him, then wiped the tears away.

"You're a good person, Pwyll," she said and hugged him tight.

"Are you going to start kissing again?" Pete asked from the mat.

"No," Pwyll said and stepped away from her.

"No?" Siobhan looked at him with that twist on her lips again.

"When it makes me want to tear my clothes off, or make you fall over?" Pwyll said. "It isn't like I don't want to," his own lips twisted into a grin. "but not until we figure out what it does to us."

"You're too good for your own good," Siobhan said and walked out of the house.

"You're an idiot," Pete said from where he lay on the floor.

"You're not kidding," Pwyll said and gently closed the door.

Chapter Three

The wind played with her hair as she walked toward her home. She knew she had a stupid grin on her face. She could only imagine what Pwyll felt in the park, but if it was just half of what had gone on in her, she had to admire his strength. He was a better person than Riordan, no matter that Riordan was the head Deacon of the Chapel and the principal of the school. He as much as tried to rape her. Siobhan tried to remember what happened, but she only brought up fuzzy pictures of what had occurred between her trashing her room and Pwyll calling her in the park.

She couldn't remember what she had done earlier, but she remembered every word that Pwyll told her about his father? What would it be like to live with that? Not easy she was sure. She still trusted Pwyll over Riordan any day. It didn't matter what he'd done. She knew he was a good person. He'd always been there for her. Sometime life just sucked, but it sucked less with Pwyll around.

She stood at the door and tried to get the courage to go in, but the door flew open. Her mother dragged her inside and wrapped her in a hug. Siobhan put her arms around her and thought about Pwyll's mother. She made sure to hug her ma back.

"Where have you been?" her mother asked.

"Mostly wandering around thinking," Siobhan said, "I'm sorry I worried you."

"Everything we do is because we love you," her mother said. There was a plaintive note in her voice that suggested that loving Siobhan was especially difficult. She was performing for someone. If they'd been alone, there would have been lectures even before the hug was finished. Her mother's embrace was a sweet trap and Siobhan fell for it every time. She looked around for the audience and saw Mr. Riordan in the living room drinking tea with his right hand while his left hand sat bandaged carefully, in full view on his knee. She could only see her father in profile, but there was a tension in his body that suggested he was holding back some strong emotion, probably shame. Her parents were all about shame, theirs, hers, the church's.

"Come in and sit down," Mr. Riordan said. Siobhan had little choice, her mother pushed her toward the living room. Siobhan reluctantly sat in her grandmother's chair. It was the only thing from Ireland in the house; that and a rock from her apparently witch aunt. She felt a chill from the rock in her pocket and resisted putting her hand on it to see if it would send chill or warmth. The chair was the most uncomfortable thing she'd ever tried to sit in. It was too low to the ground, and the seat was at an odd angle that meant she had to brace her legs to keep from sliding out of it onto the floor. The back

was lumpy with a big carving in the centre of it that meant you couldn't lean against the back.
Horsehair poked through the worn fabric to make her itch. No matter how many layers she wore it always found her skin.

She was all too familiar with the chair. It was the place she had to sit while being corrected. Siobhan had perfected the art of sitting and looking normal, if not comfortable. The goal was to try to sit in a way that made the least contact with the chair. She imagined hovering over the thing. She faced Mr. Riordan. She didn't smile, but she wasn't swearing at him, or sucking the energy from him like a crazy Irish vampire. That would have to do.

"You removed the dye from your hair," Mr. Riordan said, "that is a start. It is unfortunate that you cut your hair. A woman's hair is her honour." Siobhan thought of all the times she had been told that cutting her hair was a sin. That was odd as most of the women in the church had shorter hair than she had now, but she was the Pastor's Daughter, a rare and dangerous creature. She was supposed to somehow live by all those stupid rules that men found in the Bible for women. Nobody bothered about the rules for the men, but they would break the rules anyways.

"I have told your parents that I won't press charges, this time," Mr. Riordan held up his hand, the bandaged one, "but there must be consequences for your actions. I had to argue strongly to convince the Deacon to not simply terminate our relationship with your father." He gave Siobhan a look that made her think of him hissing in her ear that he controlled her father's future. She wasn't sure that it would work or she'd have tried to suck him dry and risk her parents immediately trying to stone her as a witch.

Somewhere between Pwyll's home and here, the power had left her. Now, she was just a teenager with a stone in her coat pocket. She couldn't call up those expressions that had given her control over Riordan and even Pwyll. Even if she did manage it, her mother would do worse than stoning her.

"We will start with the rock you used to smash my hand," Riordan said and put his good hand out. She saw the same look in his eyes as she did just before he took her into his office. Desire, she knew now. Barely controlled and overwhelming his fear. He desired that stone the same way he desired power over her. If she gave it to him, he might leave her alone. She didn't really want it. Now that it was absent, the power the stone had given her made her uncomfortable, embarrassed. She pulled it out of her pocket. It sat ice cold and inert in her hand. She could have hit him with it, but nothing else.

It isn't fair. I am not even sure what it is or what it does. My aunt's letter is gone and now the rock is gone. She put it into his hand and felt a snap like a spark from a too dry carpet. She lost her focus on the chair and fell to the floor. The room whirled for a bit, while Riordan talked some blather about the rock being possessed. Cursed, he said, like the rock that Cain used against Abel. But she was freed from its power. Now that he had the stone, he couldn't get out of the house fast enough.

"I'll leave whatever other punishment you deem suitable to you as parents," he said as he put the stone in his suit pocket and showed himself out.

"Go to your room," her mother said. "I can't believe what you've done. Don't think by washing the stain from your hair that you've washed it from your soul." She pointed up the stairs as if Siobhan might have forgotten the path to her own room.

"It might have been better if they had fired me," her father was saying as she left, "how will I face them tomorrow?" Siobhan fled before either of them thought to ask her the question. Her parents had cleaned up the glass from the mirror in the hall, but they hadn't touched her room.

She walked into her room and the destruction hit her like a blow. It felt like something evil had happened. For a second she thought about Riordan saying that the stone was cursed, but then she remembered the feel of his hands and the taste of him trying to force his kisses on her and pushed the idea from her head. *What is his excuse?* she wondered as she snuck down the stairs to find a broom and cleaning supplies. She heard her parents talking and made sure she didn't interrupt.

The broom was an old one from the basement and the bristles made a scratching sound on the floor that spoke to her of cleansing. She used the dustpan to scrape glass into the garbage.

"You'd be better spending the time in contemplation of your sin," her mother said from the doorway.

"If I'm not going to track bloody footprints through the house, I need to sweep up the glass. 'sides, cleaning up the mess is contemplative enough, and it doesn't hurt my knees."

"What is a little pain when it comes to your soul?"

"Why would God want me to spend so much time on my knees that I can't do anything else? Knees were made for more than kneeling."

Her mother started to walk into the room, but Siobhan stopped her.

"I haven't swept there yet, and I don't want your blood in my room. I will make you a deal, Mom." Siobhan said as she swept the room a second time. "I will keep my questions about God to myself, and you can keep your answers to yourself."

"What?" her mother stepped forward, then stopped and winced. Siobhan sighed.

"I'll help you to the bed," she said, "then get the glass out."

She found a pair of tweezers in the bathroom and returned to find her mother peering at the bottom of her foot while blood dripped to the floor.

"It just started bleeding," her mother said, "I didn't do anything."

"You stepped on glass, Mom." Siobhan said. "That counts as something."

She knelt in front of her mother and took her foot in her hands. She had to feel around for the glass while her mother moaned and said some words in Irish for which Siobhan was certain she was never getting a translation. When she found the glass, it was hard to get a good grip on the sliver.

Come on, she thought from habit, *a little help here?* Then she shook her head. She was so done with that. Siobhan set her jaw and fished in until her mother almost screamed, then pulled the sliver out. She put the sliver on the pile of glass that hadn't made it to the garbage can yet and found her old first aid kit from camp. A gauze pad and some tape made her mom's foot stop bleeding, but Siobhan was worried.

"That's deep, Mom," she said, "You should go to emerge and get it looked at."

"I'll take you, Marion," her dad said from the door. His voice sounded like it was the hardest thing imaginable for him to do so. *Maybe it is, it can't be easy trying to be perfect for everyone.*

"Thanks, Dad," she said and helped her mother over to where her father could take over. To her surprise, he lifted her mother easily and carried her away down the hall.

Siobhan went back to cleaning.

"I get the feeling that if I was waiting for you to undress, I'd be waiting a while." The little grey man stood on the wreck of the dresser and leered at her. For someone who wouldn't stand higher than her waist, he looked very threatening. Siobhan swiped at him with the broom but he didn't budge.

"It will take more than a whisk to shift me," the man said. He jumped off the dresser and walked to the pile of glass. He stared at it a second then picked out the sliver Siobhan had pulled from her mother's foot. "This will make a fair curse," he said and licked it.

"You leave Mom alone!" Siobhan said and snatched at him. The man jumped out of her reach.

"We could make her bleed until she was dry, or maybe put fire in the wound and burn her up?"

Siobhan's stomach heaved like she was going to puke, but the awful man would just laugh at her. She focused on the heat in her gut and felt her hair move in a breeze that wasn't there.

"I said," she grabbed him by the throat, "leave my mother alone!"

"You don't have the stone," the man said and stuck his tongue out at her, "you can't make me."

He stabbed her in the hand with the sliver, but Siobhan just tightened her grip.

"Ok," the man said, "bring the stone to the standing rock by the dawn of the full moon and she'll be fine."

Siobhan growled and tightened her grip, but the grey man grimaced at her and mouthed his words. *Kill me and your mother dies.* Siobhan screamed in frustration and threw the man at the window. He vanished before he hit it, but she heard his voice.

"I'll take that as a yes, then."

Siobhan tried to come up with a plan to get the stone back from Riordan, but the only thing she could think of was asking. As much as she loved her mother, Siobhan didn't think she could pay the only price that Riordan would ask of her. It wouldn't be just once either. She'd become little better than a slave.

The glass went into the bucket and she piled the pieces of chair and dresser in a corner. She'd need a box for that. Her clothes were torn and stained so she tossed most of them into a pile with the wood. It looked like she was wearing black for a while.

"Siobhan," her father stood in the door. He'd refused to enter her room as soon as she began puberty, as if he trusted himself so little around her.

"How's Mom?" she asked.

"They're keeping her in," he said. "Her foot wouldn't stop bleeding and they want to do more tests." He sighed, "it's a test, and we'll meet it with prayer.

"Why is everything a test?" Siobhan said. "Why do we have to fight so hard to live so miserably?"

"It is God's way," her father said, "man is made for trouble as sparks fly upward."

"That isn't good enough!" she said. Her father stood up straight like she'd slapped him, but the weight of his life pulled him down again and he left her alone. She scratched her hand absently and came away with her other hand covered in blood. How much blood could she loose through that little stab wound?

"No," Soiban said. She dug down to find the anger that had trashed the room. The power that had twisted Mr. Riordan's hand, the fire that had kept her wandering in a blizzard as if it were a sunny day. It was far, far way, almost beyond reach. Almost. She took hold of it and held it in her hand, then pushed it into the bleeding cut. "Heal," she said, "I'm not going to walk around with a bloody hand." The heat went into her like lightning and sent a shock wave through her system. She staggered and fell on the bed and gasped for air. Her skin was barely able to hold the waves of energy that crashed through her. She lost consciousness without knowing if it had even worked.

Siobhan dreamed she walked through a storm, but instead of snow it was ice that rained down. She couldn't touch anything without hitting the glass like surface of the ice. Her body was naked. It was needful. She wasn't sure what she meant by needful, but she didn't get time to think about it. She saw Pwyll's little brother lying on the black rock with his dog beside him. They were coated with ice. She started banging on the ice trying to break it and crying. Pwyll would never forgive her, but the ice just got thicker. She realized that her tears were making it impenetrable. Siobhan looked at her hands resting on the boy and she could see through them. She was ice, all of her was ice.

Siobhan woke up with a gasp and felt the cold pierce her throat. Her dream was real!

"Wait, wait," Pwyll's voice was in her ear. How would she tell him Pete was frozen in ice?

"Wake up!" Pwyll said and shook her.

"What are-" his hand covered her mouth and blocked the rest of what she was going to shout at him.

"Shhhh," he said, "don't want to wake your parents."

She decided that if he was going to muzzle her that she'd bite him. She caught a bit of his flesh in her teeth and bore down.

"Please," he said, "I won't hurt you, but you can't scream."

Siobhan gave up trying to chew through his hand and nodded. He let go of her and she punched him in the gut, then kicked him over as he crouched in pain. The window was open and snow was drifting across the remains of her desk. She closed the window, then she closed the door.

"So," she said, "what is going on? Did you decide that one kiss meant you could climb into my room and take the rest of me?"

"That's the last thing I want," Pwyll said.

Siobhan felt her face form *that* expression, the one that had sent Riordan out of control.

"Really," she said.

"Look," he said, "I enjoyed the kiss and all, but it was just a kiss. There's a long path from a kiss on the road to a kiss between the sheets." He sat up and groaned softly. "It's something my grandfather used to say. I wish it was something my Ma had listened to, but that's not important."

"What is important enough to break into my room in the middle of the night?"

"The stone," Pwyll said, "do you still have it?"

"How do you know about the stone?"

"Do you still have it?"

"No, Riordan took it. How do you know about the stone?"

"Your aunt's letter," Pwyll pulled the crumple of papers from his pocket.

Siobhan snatched them and smoothed them out.

"That's mine!" she said, "You've been reading my mail?" She ignored whatever he was trying to say as an excuse and bent over the letter. It was too dark to see. Then a white glow illuminated the letter. *Well, at least he was a little useful. As long as he holds the flashlight and keeps his mouth shut.*

"Siobhan?" her door swung open and her father put his head into the room.

"It's Ok, Dad," she said, "I can explain."

"Not only the Whore of Babylon," he said, "but a witch." He stepped into the room and raised his hand to strike her.

"Not now," Siobhan said. "I don't have time for this, just go away and forget you ever saw me." A twinge ran from her shoulder to her hand and a spark jumped to strike her father's heart. He put his hand out in supplication, but then dropped it. He walked out of the room leaving the door open. She heard him go down the stairs and open the front door.

"What is he doing?"

"What you told him to do," Pwyll said. "Read the letter, it will explain."

"Where's the flashlight?"

"What flashlight?"

"The one you were shining on the letter for me."

"That wasn't me, Siobhan." He pointed at her hand.

There was a tiny star shaped scar where the little grey man had stabbed her. It shone with a soft white light.

Chapter Four

The stone in Mr. Riordan's pocket whispered to him. *The witch should burn; her hair is already aflame.* He knew better than to pay much attention to the stone. Things whispered to him all the time. It was a cheat and a snare. A trap of the devil, but her hair was like a flame. His hand ached with the vision of her hair. She'd burned him with that fire and lied to him. He should have fired her father and sent them far away. But that hair, that skin, even the fire of her lips as he kissed her. God would forgive him. God had forgiven him before and they weren't nearly as beautiful, as deadly.

At home his wife was waiting at the door as she was supposed to. She was a good woman, a godly woman, a boring woman. She hadn't borne him any sons, but people didn't understand the need for sons in this time.

"Do you need anything, Dear?" his wife said.

"No, go to bed," Riordan said. He couldn't sleep with his wife while the flame burned in his mind. It wouldn't be right. He went into his study and closed the door but didnt lock it. He didn't need to. Clara would never enter this room. He'd told her not to.

He put the stone on the desk and peered at it. Ordinary black rock, it had no glint, no colour, nothing to distinguish it from any other piece of granite. He picked the stone up again. It felt

47

heavier than it should, smoother, fitting in his hand perfectly to strike someone. Just as the girl had struck him. He tore the bandages from his wounded hand. It lay twisted and black on the desk mocking him with its weakness. *No one with a blemish shall go before the Lord* the Book said. He picked up the rock to smash his hand. *If your hand causes you to sin, the Lord said, strike it from you.* The stone hit his hand, but it didn't crush. There was no weight, no hardness. It felt like flesh to his blackened fingers like the softness under *her* clothes. The softness she used to trap him.

He left the stone in his ruined hand. He breathed harder, faster, it was pulling him in. The fire, the flame, her hair, soft places calling out for him. He shouted and his head snapped back against his chair. His breath rasped from his chest. His heart thumped. He clutched the stone with his twisted flesh and let the ecstasy wash through him. He no longer ignored the whispers. They were in his ear like a lover's breath.

He would have her. He had to have her, and she would burn. They both would burn with this fire. His mind filled with the vision and it was all he saw.

Chapter Five

Siobhan stared at her hand and the light went out. She squeaked and fell back into Pwyll who caught her and held her safe. Only she was mad at him. He'd broken into her room in the middle of the night, and her Dad had caught them. Something was weird about her dad, but she needed to read this letter and figure out what was going on.

Guard it carefully, the letter said, *it is a part of your heritage.*

"Great," she said, "first paragraph and I've already blown it."

The tradition in our family is that the stone is the one Cain used to slay Abel. I don't know about that, but I know the stone does something to the person who holds it. It magnifies whatever they are feeling. The results can be devastating. We aren't designed to hold such feelings, yet it is addictive. It is our task as Siobhan to hold the stone and keep the balance. It is such a small thing, yet small things change the balance. A grain of sand can tip a balance.

You must learn to master yourself. If I'd been allowed to train you it would be easier, but you have mother's chair. It will have to do.

"What does Grandmother's chair have to do with anything?"

If you don't master your emotions, you could do great damage. The stone magnifies emotion, but it also acts as a focus for the power you carry within you. That power is just power. It is clear as water and as pure, but what you add to water can make a healing tea, or a deadly potion.

There are times when it is useful to have such focused power, but dangerous too. Other people may be weak and hear words spoken with power as curses or spells, some will fear them, others crave them. Be mindful of what you speak because your words may cause unintended damage. Damage that is impossible to repair. You can no more take back your words than catch a stone that you've thrown.

"Dad," Siobhan said, "I have to find Dad. I told him to go away."

"Read the letter first," Pwyll said, "then I'll help you find your Dad."

The light flickered, but Siobhan took a deep breath and turned back to the words on the letter.

I wish I could travel to you, but that is impossible. God has a different trip in mind for me and it is long overdue. The stone sometimes manifests as if it has a will of its own. Some hear whispers that speak to their desires, some see things, totems that talk to them and make bargains. Whatever you do, make no bargain with the stone. It will hold you to every letter of the bargain and make you regret it for all the days of your life. Yet if you do, you must fulfill your end, however painful, or the stone will own you, body and soul.

"Could I have done any worse?" Siobhan said. "I've lost the stone, made a bargain with that little man and cursed my father."

"You finished the letter?"

"Yeah, it stops with the stone owning me, body and soul."

"Your aunt didn't sign it or anything?"

"No, it just stops."

"Those were all the pages that your mom gave me. It was strange like she couldn't stand to touch them. When you left, I hung my coat up and went to bed. I had this freaky dream that you turned to ice and broke when I tried to kiss you. I wanted to make sure you were Ok. I found the letter when I put my hand in my coat pocket. It read it to see what freaked your mom out."

"I guess having a witch as a sister would do it," Siobhan said, "I've always thought that Mom wanted a boy not a girl. You couldn't name a boy Siobhan, could you?"

"So let's go find your Dad."

"We should find the last part of the letter, maybe it has the answer. Please?"

Siobhan watched as Pwyll sighed, then sat still. When she prayed, she tried to sit still, but her hands moved or she shifted her weight. Pwyll was so still, she could barely see him breathing. He looked empty, like he wasn't truly there. "What are you doing?" she said and poked him.

"Trying to find your letter," he said, "give me a minute. I've never done this in public before."

She got up and found some clean underwear and went to the bathroom to change. Wearing underwear this long made her feel grody. It also meant she didn't need to see Pwyll sitting there empty. It was too freaky, like he sent himself out ahead and his body just sat there. She changed clothes quickly, in case he walked in on her, but when he didn't she brushed her hair. The short hair made her look strange. She was used to the weight of it on her neck and the hair covered her shoulders and breasts. Now, this odd girl looked at her in the mirror. She looked older, tougher. Like she'd lived more.

"You'd better get out there," her reflection told her. "You have no idea what's coming for you."

She gasped and ran out of the bathroom straight into Pwyll. He staggered back until he hit the wall. Her lips brushed his, and a spark leapt between them. She closed the distance again and kissed him. She felt the flow of energy between them, but she made it into a loop, whatever she took, she gave back to him. The energy still heated her and her hands went from on his chest to exploring.

Pwyll pushed her back a little.

"I really would love to do this all night," he said as his hitched his pants up. "But we don't have time. We need to find your dad."

"I thought we were looking for the letter?" Siobhan tried to push away the feelings of just a second ago. Wasn't she angry at him? Weren't the guys supposed to want this, whatever it was?

"Your dad has it, and I think he's in trouble." He put out his hand, and she clasped it. The flow was still there, but muted. They ran down the stairs together and out the door. The snow turned into rain and everything was getting coated with a thin sheet of ice. Siobhan thought of her dream and shivered, but she kept running.

She had no idea what time it was. The rain fell past streetlights forming halos. Few houses had lights on and there were no cars on the road. She might as well have been in one of those movies where everyone disappears and it was just her in the world. Only the warmth of Pwyll's hand told her that he was present. She didn't feel anyone. She hadn't since she'd kicked that horrible grey man. Somehow he'd taken her awareness of people, but how had he done that and left the energy?

She recalled the kiss in the hallway and knew the answer. He was hoping she'd get lost in the energy. Her aunt warned her about addiction. It made sense now. She pushed all awareness of the energy away but the faintest trickle to keep her connected to Pwyll.

He never wavered. When he changed directions, he used their joined hands to swing her around the corner without losing speed. They came to the top of a long hill and began to slide. Instead of fighting it, Pwyll set his feet like they were on an invisible board and slid down the hill. Siobhan tried to emulate him, but she wasn't as steady. He caught her other hand and held her up. He looked her in the eye and grinned, then he hooted at the top of his lungs and she couldn't help but scream as they picked up speed.

"You have to trust me," he said to her.

"Why? What?" she said.

"Just watch me and don't falter."

Siobhan didn't have time for any more questions. They were almost at the bottom of the hill and traffic whizzed by on the street across the bottom.

"We have to stop!" she said, but he gripped her hands.

"Trust me!"

She looked ahead and closed her eyes, expecting a car or truck to slam into her at any second. Nothing happened. She opened her eyes to see that they'd past the intersection without being hit. She looked at him and was going to say something, but he mouthed something at her, then fell to the road with her on top of him. They slowed rapidly before he hit something that made him grunt and sent her rolling away from him.

She climbed to her feet and ran back to him. He still lay on the street.

"Ooof," he said, "didn't think about stopping soon enough. Your dad is over there." He pointed from where he was lying. "I think he's hurt, he must have slid down the hill too. Go, find him. I'll be Ok."

Siobhan ran in the direction that Pwyll pointed. The pavement got rough suddenly and even with the ice her feet didn't slide. Her father lay in a heap on the road. He was still breathing, but just barely. Blood poured from a wound on his head.

"Dad," she said, lifting him to a sitting position. "Dad, I'll get you help."

His eyes opened and looked at her, but there was nothing. No frown of disappointment, no recognition.

"I must have fallen," he said. "Thank you for stopping to help an old man."

"Not so old," she said.

"I feel old," he said, "I feel the weight of every year as my failure piles upon me," he tried to smile and ended with an awful grimace. "But I shouldn't be telling my woes to a stranger, not a young girl like you."

"Don't you recognize me?" Siobhan said, "It's me, it's Siobhan!"

"Sorry," he said, "I've met so many people over the years. I can't keep track of them all." To her horror, tears flowed down his cheeks. She recalled what she'd said to him, filled with light and power. *Go away and forget you ever saw me.*

She screamed with the pain of her heart breaking, and turned the scream into a word to send it up into the uncaring night.

"Help!"

People came from the cross street. They were shouting and slipping on the ice. Cars with flashing lights appeared and then finally an ambulance. They took her dad from her arms and put him in the ambulance.

"Thanks for your help, miss," her dad said as they lifted him in. She wanted to climb in with him, but she couldn't find the words she needed to explain how she was the daughter of a man who didn't know her. They drove away and left her in the dark with a police officer and her partner.

"Can you tell us what happened?" she asked.

"We were sliding down the hill," she said.

"We?" the officer had her book out and was writing carefully.

"My...boyfriend and I. It took us by surprise." She looked over to where Pwyll should have been sitting rubbing his side a little. All she could see was a darker patch on the pavement.

"I'm so sorry," the officer said, "we didn't know he was your friend. We're so sorry."

Siobhan hadn't thought anything could hurt worse than holding her father while he didn't remember her. Because she had cursed him.

This was worse. Pwyll had died on the road alone while she ignored him. Didn't even think of him. Sobs tore at her throat as she ran to the dark patch. The cops tried to stop her and she heard herself snarl like an animal. One cop flinched and Siobhan pulled herself away. She ignored the cold on her knees and put her hand on Pwyll's blood. The grey man had said blood could be used to curse, and he was killing her mother with it.

Maybe it could heal.

The blood had just the tiniest hint of his energy left. She pulled everything she had. Everything she was and sent it in an arrow to chase down Pwyll and somehow make him whole. It wasn't until she let the arrow fly that she thought she should have kept something for herself.

Chapter Six

She lay face down on the road and the ice seeped into her soul. The cold felt good. It dulled the pain, it pushed her thoughts away. The cops were talking.

"How was I to know she'd collapse on us? The bus hasn't made it to the hospital yet. All the rest are busy."

"We could load her into the car."

"Yeah, and if she dies, it's all on us. Damn this full moon stupidity, and we still have another five hours on this shift."

"Wonderful."

Footsteps crunched on the ice and a pair of boots appeared in front of her.

"Hey, she's moving!" Hands lifted her and carried her to the car. One of the cops shoved something in her pocket.

"I think this is yours," he said.

"Do you have somewhere we can take you?" the female cop asked.

"Yeah," Siobhan said, "home isn't far from here." She gave them the address, and the cops drove carefully through the icy streets to drop her off in front of her house.

"Stay inside until the ice is gone," one of them said.

She walked into the house and closed the door. It didn't feel like home. Not without her

Mom and Dad around. It was always them that made home with all the moves they made. This was just one more. She thought of her mom bleeding her life away in the hospital, her dad with his mind empty of her. She let her coat drop to the floor and heard a faint crackle of paper. What had the cop put in her pocket?

She pulled it out and flattened it. It was the last page of the letter from her aunt.

All this sounds dire, and I'm sure you're wondering how you will ever succeed. Siobhans have failed before, they have fallen or given in to the addiction, but they have also succeeded. They've made life better, maintained their balance. Lived with joy. Remember this; no last stands, no dying in hopeless battle. It is better to fail than die, because you can always learn from a failure. You can't learn when you're dead.

Though I've never met you, I named you for this task. I trust that you are worthy. I will be watching from wherever I go when I'm gone, to hell if the pastor has his way, but I hope to surprise him yet.

Your Aunt Siobhan

Even her aunt was dead. Had probably died before all this started. Lot of help she was. Siobhan dropped the letter to the floor.

Failure was better than death. Siobhan wasn't sure. Death looked inviting right now. She went into the living room and flopped into the closest chair. Grandmother's chair. Her back ached immediately, so she tried a different position. It was no better. It was too much work to get out of the chair and sit on the couch. So she pushed herself up and tried sitting how she had for Riordan. It took too much energy. Something she didn't have. She turned around and knelt facing the back of the chair. The carving was at eye level. It looked like an eye watching her. She'd never noticed it before.

The angle of the seat that was impossible for sitting welcomed kneeling as Siobhan was. The carved eye watched her, and she saw more and more details. Its grain looked like wrinkles in an old woman's skin. They looked like laugh lines, but the kind that are accompanied by wisdom. Siobhan had met a few women with faces like that. It comforted her that the chair didn't judge her. She felt at peace, more than she had for days, or even years. She looked into that wooden eye and wept. The arms of the chair seemed to wrap around her and hold her tight.

She climbed out of the chair and took a deep breath. The night wasn't over yet.

Dawn came late in the winter.

Some of the calm of kneeling in that chair guided Siobhan to take a shower. The running water felt a little like the energy from Pwyll. She let it soak into her. She had done what she could for her friend. Now, she needed the strength. Siobhan dried off after the shower and went digging for some different clothes. She didn't feel like wearing the black right now. Instead, she found some old jeans and a raggedy sweater. It had belonged to her mom, before Siobhan had wheedled it out of her. She went into her room and stared at the walls. The cleanup hadn't got past sweeping. The bloody mess on the walls still mocked her anger. Only it wasn't random.

She looked again and saw there was a pattern beneath the mess. It looked like odd shaped letters made of twigs. She'd seen writing like it before. There was a memorial, something about the potato famine and the town welcoming settlers. A hundred years later they'd brought a stone from Ireland and set it up in the park. The stone had this kind of writing on it. She went still and let the pieces juggle around. The writing was a warning and a barrier. A door. She'd opened a door in her rage and the grey man had come through. If she had just...

She pushed away the thought. Later, she might indulge in what ifs, but she didn't have time now. She needed to think. Why did she know about the stone? It wasn't the kind of thing they taught at the school. In fact, they would have hated it. Anything that didn't match their idea of the faith was the devil's work. Mr. Riordan had mentioned it during a service at Chapel. He'd warned the students to stay away because it was the devil's stone. Caitlin had made a joke about the shape that

Siobhan only now understood after seeing the grey man the first time waddling toward her.

That wasn't important, what was important was she knew how to get Mr. Riordan to meet her at the stone. She looked up Riordan's number in her father's book.

"Good morning, Mr. Riordan," she said when he answered the phone. "I'm sorry for bothering you so early, but my parents are both in the hospital and I need your guidance. You're the only one I could think to call. There is no one here, it wouldn't be right for you to come to the house. I'll meet you in front of the school and you can tell me what I should do."

She hung up before he could get a word in, but she heard him breathing like he'd just run a marathon. He'd be there, but she wanted to be there first. She threw on her coat and ran out the door. The ice almost sent her flying. It coated the world as it had in her dream. Siobhan pushed the thought away and headed toward the school. People were moving about trying to scrape ice off their cars and cursing the weather.

The sky shone a pewter grey in the east. She didn't have much time. Fortunately, the school wasn't far. She took the shortcut through the tiny park that faced the main doors, but stopped and waited at the black stone pillar that stood in the middle of the park. The stone was the same kind of stone that her aunt had sent her. She put her hand on it and felt the cold that went deeper than the coating of ice on the pillar.

Mr. Riordan was standing at the door of the school.

Siobhan waved and tried to put the siren call as well as her own innocence into the motion. She must have succeeded as Mr. Riordan walked across the road to her.

"I think we'd do better to talk in my office," he said. He looked terrible. His suit hung off him and his tie was askew, but his eyes burned with desire.

"Sure, Mr. Riordan," she said, "but please, may I have my stone back? I'm really sorry, I'll do anything to prove that." Siobhan felt like throwing up, but Riordan started breathing harder and he brought his left hand out of his pocket. It was clutching the stone like he wasn't able to let go of it.

"I can't let go," Mr. Riordan said. "It won't let me let go." His voice was thin and plaintive like an old man's.

"Just stretch out your arm," she said. The sun was lighting the tops of the skyscrapers she could see past the school building. "Just stretch your arm, and it will be enough."

Shaking as if the stone were the heaviest thing he'd ever lifted, Mr. Riordan reached out to her. She took the stone and he let his arm drop with a huge sigh of relief.

"Alright, I'm here, and I have the stone," she said. She ignored Riordan's puzzled look as the grey man stepped around the side of the building. He was enormous.

"Your friend has been feeding me," the grey man boomed. "Give me the stone."

"Come here and get it," she said, "you said *at the standing stone.*"

"I also said dawn," the grey man said as he thumped across the street.

"The light isn't on the stone yet," Siobhan said. She gave him the stone just before the sun lit the top of the stone.

"Your mother will live," the grey man said, "but she will curse you for saving her." He backhanded her. Siobhan rolled across the icy park with the heat of the blow on her face. The grey man was laughing as he stomped toward the pillar. What would happen if he connected that stone to the pillar? *Nothing good*, Siobhan thought. She ran at the grey man. He obviously thought she was defeated because he didn't even look at her. Not until she hit his feet with her best illegal soccer tackle. He hit the ground as she rolled away. Now, he noticed her. He roared rage at her and tried to crush her with his feet. She kept rolling, pulling him further away from the pillar. Then he switched tactics and grabbed her by the throat. He lifted her up and let her dangle from his hand.

"It would have been so much easier to just give me what I wanted," he said. "That's not such a big thing, is it? He had no problem." The grey man pointed to where Riordan sat gasping air and watching them with his mouth hanging up. He looked like he was dying.

"I'm taking back my kick," Siobhan said. "They aren't dead."

"What?" The grey man slammed her into the pillar. She felt the ice run under her skin. It pulled her will from her. The sunlight lost its glow as the world began to turn grey.

"He," she pointed at Riordan, "he's still alive, my mother's still alive, my father's alive. The deal was my kick for their death." The grey man's hand was choking the life from her, but she forced the words past the barrier in her throat.

"That can be fixed," the grey man made a fist with the other hand. He was big enough now he could reach across to Riordan.

"Too late," Siobhan said. She took hold of the energy that flowed around her, sensing Riordan's exhaustion and self-disgust, and the students who were beginning to show up at the school. The ice of the pillar exploded into flame and colour returned to the world. The flame pushed the grey man's hand from her throat. His presence still blotted out much of the light, but she felt past him to something she hadn't noticed missing.

Thanks for coming, she thought toward the sunlit sky. She heard the light laughing, and breathed energy into a web around the grey man.

"Why are you saving this creep?" the grey man said as he stretched toward Riordan, but his arms were too short to reach now., "He was going to rape you. You know that."

"His life isn't mine to take," Siobhan said.

"... and your father isn't even going to remember you," the grey man squeaked as he looked up at her.

"That isn't his fault, is it?" she said.

"Your mother hates you and fears you," the little man shouted from under the stone crushing him to the ground. Siobhan bent over and picked up the stone.

"She named me Siobhan."

The grey man vanished.

"You're a witch," Riordan said.

"You're a rapist," Siobhan said, "it isn't illegal to be a witch."

A police car pulled up.

"We got a call about a giant naked man running around." the officer said. "Would you be able to tell me about that?"

"This man needs to face his crimes," Siobhan said, pointing at Mr. Riordan. "He tried to rape me yesterday."

"You *Jezebel*," Mr. Riordan yelled at her, "God has forgiven me."

"Yes," Siobhan said, "she has, but that is the beginning, not the end of making it right."

Mr. Riordan kept yelling at her, so the officers told him to stop. Then he yelled at the officers. They were putting him in the car as she went back through the shortcut.

The morning warmed the pavement and melted the ice as Siobhan walked toward the hospital. A million scenarios ran through her head as she walked. Her mother was dead after all, her father broken. Or maybe they would know somehow that she had saved them and they would never bother her again. She'd figure out how to fix her dad's memory and everything would be perfect.

She walked in the light and knew that none of it was true. She couldn't fix her dad. In just a second of carelessness, she'd shattered that relationship. It was gone. It wasn't his fault. She would just have to start over.

Her mother was harder, full of more hard edges. Her mother who hates witches, but named her daughter after a witch. She thought for a moment of curses, but pushed it away. She didn't have the right. They would work it out, maybe, probably even. She would have to see. They had time.

She reached the hospital and observed the people going in and out the doors. They wove dances in the light and energy. Some receiving, some giving. She heaved a sighed and walked across the road and through the main doors.

"Hi," she said, "my mother came in yesterday with a bleeding foot. They admitted her. Her name is Marion O'Hullan."

The woman directed her to a room where her mother sat white between white sheets.

"Hello," Siobhan said.

"Hello," her mother said.

"How's the foot?"

"Stopped bleeding."

Siobhan looked at her mother, then went over and hugged her.

"I am glad you're OK," she said, "really."

"Your father's lost his memory," her mother said. "They brought him in and he barely recognized me. He can't remember much after you were born. They say it is a bump on the head."

"The bump on the head didn't help," Siobhan said.

"Like your aunt then?"

Siobhan shrugged.

"You know, when we lived in Ireland your Grandmother was deathly afraid of spiders. One day Siobhan told her they were cute little pets. Grandmother wouldn't hear of killing spiders after that. She was still afraid, but she couldn't bear to think of hurting them, they were so cute."

They sat in silence for a while.

Her father walked in with a bandage around his head.

"You must be the daughter Marion told me about, Siobhan."

"That's right, Dad."

"It's funny, I can't remember you at all."

"It's Ok, we'll make more memories."

He nodded and sat beside her mom. He wasn't bent over from shame anymore. He sat straight and at ease. *Maybe I did him a favour, maybe I really was the cause of his shame all those years.*

"Siobhan," her dad said, "I remember you were there last night and helped me. I didn't know who you were then. I want to tell you that I'm proud of you. I want you to know that my first memory of you is being grateful that you were there."

"Thanks, Dad." Siobhan left her parents together while she sat in the hall and wept silently. She'd hoped that winning would erase all the pain. It didn't. She sighed and pushed the tears from her face with her hands. A nurse handed her a tissue.

"It's always hard when they can't remember," she said, "families are caught between hoping for the memories to come back, and hoping the bad ones stay forgotten. Whatever comes back, comes back." she said.

Siobhan went back out to the main desk.

"I'm looking for a friend who came in last night?" she said. "His name is Pwyll Jones."

"Sorry," the woman said, "he's no longer with us."

Siobhan turned and walked away. Once more the tears washed her face, and she let them. Pwyll deserved nothing less. She went and sat on the bench across the road. She could see now, between her tears the threads that were worry, or joy or grief. Life went on. She let the morning carry her away. So, she thought, before she let thought go too, this is how Pwyll did it.

She wasn't sure how long she was gone, or where she went, but when she came back, Siobhan could feel the warmth of another person on the bench,

"Good morning," the person said, and Siobhan gasped and looked at him.

"Pwyll!" she said. "They told me you weren't with them and I thought..."

"Almost," he said, "I was just floating, wondering how I was supposed to help you from wherever I was, when this bolt hit me. I was back in the ambulance and scared the liver out of the attendant who thought I died. They checked me over and released me. I went home to make sure Pete and Brac were Ok," he grinned a little. "I came to find you. I heard something about the police being at your school and I got worried."

"It got a little crazy," Siobhan said, "but it worked out all right." She turned to look at Pwyll. She could see the energy move within him, within the people around her. She sensed the pattern that guided the flow. Siobhan looked up and grinned at the sunlight.

"I'm a witch, you know," she said to Pwyll and the sunlight.

"I know," Pwyll said, "I can live with that." He smiled at her. "I was hoping for another dose."

Siobhan wrapped her arms around him and kissed him. She didn't try to control the energy, she just let it move from him to her, from her to him, from them to the sky.

Strange Carnivores

Alex McGilvery

Strange Carnivores

Strange Carnivores

Chapter One

"Don't go into the swamp!" The girl behind the counter looked at me with concern leaking through her goth makeup. She was the fourth, or maybe the fifth, person to warn me. It depends on whether you count the guys at the gas station as one person or two. I smiled and picked up my bag of groceries and headed out to my car. I wasn't sure whether it was real concern about my competence as a woman, or they just didn't like the swamp. It didn't matter to me either way and it wasn't going to change my plans.

Heat hit me as I stepped out the door. I'd walked into walls that had less force. The bag of last minute supplies went in the back alongside the eight cases of bottled water. I pulled a bottle out and climbed into my truck. The AC banished the sticky heat and I headed out of town.

My guide told me his name was Bubba. I'd asked him if he played banjo. He'd been hurt by the question and I had to let him talk his fee up another ten percent before he agreed to let me come. I wasn't the one footing the bill so I didn't care. My agent heard rumours about rumours of strange things in that very swamp that the locals warned me against. I made my living taking pictures of rumours. A swamp didn't scare me.

Bubba's place was a half hour out of town. As least that's what he'd told me. It took me an hour and a half and I had to winch my truck out of two holes in what he called a road. I finally wheeled into the yard and parked. There, was the biggest damn vehicle I'd seen outside a monster truck show.

I walked around the beast and shook my head in wonder. The tires were taller than I was. Good thing that my hind brain was paying attention while I was drooling over Bubba's truck. It had me up the ladder that was welded beside the driver's door and sitting in the truck bed before my front brain spotted the two immense dogs creeping up on me.

From my perch, I admired their collars with the three inch spikes. The dogs were grey and their skin hung loose on them. My good camera was in the truck with the rest of my gear, but I took some shots of them with my iPhone. The one of the bigger dog with its paws on the side of the truck growling at me was particularly nice. Once it had sniffed in my general direction the dog lay down on the dirt of Bubba's yard and apparently went to sleep. I figured the other one was lying on the other side of the truck.

With it not being polite to investigate under the tarp I sat on, I amused myself for a while taking pictures of the rest of Bubba's yard. After I'd exhausted the limited angles from the truck bed, I chipped away at the mud to find out what the original colour of the thing was. As far as I could tell it was painted mud colour.

Bubba came out as I was half way through a collection of pictures of mosquitos biting me. He looked to be not much older than me, but in much better shape. The jeans and t-shirt were ragged, but showed off a trim shape. He stretched, ambled over to a bush and peed on it. The smaller dog wandered over and sniffed at the bush, then he lifted his leg and peed on it too. The dog that was lying pretending to be asleep looked up at me as if to say 'men, what can you do?'. To be honest, by this point I was ready to find my own bush.

"Hey," Bubba said, after he'd stretched again, "what are you doing up there?"

"Waiting for you," I said, "the dogs suggested it."

"These two?" he said. "They wouldn't hurt a fly." The bitch dog jumped up and snapped at a fly that had bit her rear. I just raised my eyebrow, but I climbed down off the truck. The dogs came over and sniffed at me a little. One sneezed, then they walked over to the porch and flopped down. Some leaves and dust wafted down on them.

"So," Bubba said, "you must be Sally."

"Yup," I grabbed my camera bag from the truck. "Do you mind?" He waved at me and I started shooting background shots of his place. If it weren't for the monstrous truck, it could have passed as a hillbilly cabin from a hundred years ago. The house sat   a little crooked, and the porch crooked the other way. The chimney leaned a third direction. No two windows were the same size or at the same level in the wall. A fence enclosed a small garden with chickens that hopped through the boards to find food on either side. I could smell a pig somewhere.

"When you're done," Bubba said, "come on in and we'll talk." He climbed the steps to the porch and walked between the dogs to go back into the house. I heard some clanking of pots and decided I'd give him a little more time to clean up. There was an interesting looking flower just a little way under the trees, but when I went to photograph it I felt a hot breath on my hand and the bitch dog stood between me and the trees.

OK," I said to the dog, and scratched her behind the ears, "thanks for the warning." She padded away around the cabin, so I followed her. The pig was there; a big sow with a litter of weanlings. She huffed at me, but the fence around her looked much stronger than the garden fence so I ignored her. The dog was sniffing at another of the flowers I'd seen. This one was in the sun. I was soon lost in getting macro shots of the flower and the astonishing assortment of insects that crawled all over it.

The dog licked my hand after a bit and we walked back around the cabin. I went in the door while she lay down, bringing more leaves and dust from the rafters. The dirt yard and gargantuan truck were still there when I looked out the door. Wanted to make sure I hadn't been transported to a different dimension. The inside of the cabin was decorated in immaculate french provincial. The walls were covered with art that had to be original. It ran the gamut from abstract to a pointillist rendering of the flower I'd just been shooting that looked like a photograph until I got close enough to see the dots.

Bubba laughed and handed me a glass of red wine. I sipped at it and was wasn't surprised to taste one of the nicest Cabernet Sauvignons I'd ever had. He toasted me with his glass and sat in a chair that utterly clashed with his tattered overalls.

"Protective camouflage," he said, "the dogs make sure that no one comes into the house that I don't invite. So it's safe to indulge myself."

"I feel privileged," I said, sipped at the wine and put my camera on the table. He picked it up and glanced at me. I nodded and took another sip. Bubba looked through the pictures, stopping now and again to peer more closely at one.

"Nice," he said, "you've got a good eye and great sense of light and shade." He put the camera down on the table and picked up his own wine. "I think you'll do just fine. Mars and Diana like you too."

"The dogs of war?" I looked out the door at them.

"They are as close as I could find to the battle dogs the Romans used."

"They're massive."

"Mastiffs," Bubba said, "born and bred for battle. The big ones the Romans had could bring down a horse."

"These are small ones?" I couldn't help the squeak in my voice. Diana lifted her head and panted at me.

"Smaller anyway," Bubba said. "You hungry? I've got a beef brisket that is just dying to go with the wine."

"Sounds great," I said and was soon tucking into melt-in-my-mouth beef with tiny potatoes on the side and a salad of greens from the garden with a dressing which tied the whole meal together. As we ate, the light faded until Bubba lit a lantern and hung it on a hook. The cabin became an intimate bubble of light.

"Well," I said as I pushed myself away from the table and let Bubba pour a little more wine in my glass, "you are the most interesting redneck I've ever met. Is your name really Bubba?"

He winced and I wondered if my question had set me up for another ten percent on the fee.

"My full name is William Robert Spencer," he said. "The kids at school called me Billy Bob and it got shortened to Bubba. It isn't pretty, but it's a name."

The dogs were on their feet and growling so low I half expected my fillings to pop from my teeth. There were shadows moving out in the yard.

Impossibly fast, they left human shaped after images.

"Our guests have arrived," Bubba said. "Don't worry, the dogs won't let them in."

"Let what in?" I asked as I picked up my camera and started shooting through the door. I was flipping through setting to find one that would be a good balance between focus and speed and only paying partial attention to my host.

"The vampires," he said, as one shadow stopped briefly at the step before vanishing away into the night.

I stared at him in disbelief, but then looked at my camera to see what it had captured. All I could see was red eyes, glistening fangs and a white ruffled shirt.

"Vampires?" I said.

"Worse pests than mosquitoes," Bubba said and poured more wine into my glass. "I'll tell you about it in the morning."

I wanted answers right now, but my experience told me that I'd get the answers when he was ready to give them to me.

Chapter Two

After a couple more glasses of wine, I allowed Bubba to show me to his room. He was going to sleep on the couch. Diana parked herself at the foot of the bed. Even in my blurred state I knew that nothing was going to get past her.

I dreamed of vampires.

Actually one vampire. His name was Francisco Medea and he'd explored with Juan Ponce de Leon. Francisco spoke lovely Spanish that somehow I could understand. He'd been waiting for me for five hundred years. I was his soulmate, his completion. We walked through a sunlit forest.

"You have nothing to fear," he said. "Give yourself to me and we will be together for eternity." His thumb rubbed the inside of my wrist and my breathing quickened. His fingers fastened in my hair and tilted my head back. I waited for the pain of his fangs in my neck, but strangely I felt them in my arm. "Come." Francisco was getting annoyed. I didn't want him angry at me, but I had to wonder why he was biting my arm.

Francisco bared his fangs, but not at me; it was something behind me. I heard the deep rumbling growl that the dogs had used to greet the vampire's visit. The vampire snarled something that was not Castilian Spanish and vanished into the night.

82

I woke standing in the door of my room. Diana had my arm held firmly in her mouth.

"I'm OK now," I said to her. She let go of my arm and a faint line of blood dripped from where her fangs had pierced my arm. She hung her head and whined, but I dropped to my knees and hugged her tight.

"You did what you had to do, Diana," I said. Tears ran down my face and disappeared into her grey fur. She turned her head and licked my face then padded down the hall to where Bubba slept on the couch. She gave a single soft woof, and Bubba was instantly awake. He saw the blood on my arm and smacked himself in the head.

"Damn, I should have been more careful." He rolled out of bed and walked to the kitchen to pull out a box. He turned back to me holding the box when he realized that he had no clothes on. I could see him debating modesty or expediency.

"It's a little late to worry about it now," I said, "besides, it is a very effective distraction from the pain."

Bubba shrugged and waved me to a kitchen chair. Mars padded in carrying a pair of pants which Bubba pulled on. He took my arm and dusted it with something that looked like crushed moss, while the dogs lay and watched intently.

"What is that stuff?" I asked him.

"Spanish moss," he said, "it helps to stop the bleeding and controls infection."

I saw some other things in his first aid kit and decided that I wasn't going to ask any more questions. He wrapped my arm in soft white cotton instead of the snake skin and put the kettle on to heat. When the water boiled, he crushed something into a mug and poured water over it. He added honey and milk then pushed the mug over to me. I sipped at it and lifted my eyebrows. I'd expected something herby and perhaps bitter, but it had a faint sour taste that balanced with the honey. I had no problem drinking the cup to the bottom.

Bubba took my hand and led me back to the bedroom. He tucked me in and gave me a kiss on the forehead. I was asleep before his lips left my skin.

The sunlight in my eyes woke me. I tried to remember the last time I had wakened without the buzz of an alarm clock. Bubba was waiting in the kitchen with a cup of coffee in his hands and a bemused look on his face.

"I'm guessing last night wasn't just a dream," I said as I looked at my bandaged arm.

"You came under a mental attack from a vampire."

"Francisco Medea." I found a mug in the dish drainer and poured myself a coffee.

Bubba shook his head.

"I got careless," he said, "I should have warned you about the possibility and warded you better."

"No harm done," I said, "and the night wasn't all bad." I laughed as Bubba turned red. "I am comforted actually, that you thought first about my safety and second about your modesty."

Bubba laughed and relaxed. We drank our coffee in silence. He poured us both a second cup then busied himself cooking breakfast. The dogs came in and flopped under the table as he put a plate in front of me. The food was as good as the meal the night before.

"So," Bubba said as he drained the last of his coffee, "are you ready?"

"It's what I came for." I got up to fetch my camera bag and found Diana at my elbow with the bag hanging from her jaws. "Thank you, Diana," I said and rubbed her head. I couldn't imagine how just yesterday I thought she was scary. The bag went over my shoulder and I pulled the camera out to check the battery and card. "All set."

Bubba led the way to the truck. I climbed the ladder and got in the driver's side and slid over to the passenger seat where I fastened the five-point harness. Bubba was in and done up before I'd finished.

"I'm rather impressed that you made it through with that little truck of yours." He spun the wheels and we headed back down the road. The truck splashed through the second place that I had to winch out of, then we turned to follow a faint track between the trees.

I'd started out by admiring the sheer size and power of Bubba's truck, but by the time I got the first whiff of swamp I was in awe of his driving skill. He drove smoothly and in control all the time, even as we crawled over fallen trees or left a rooster tail through a deep hole.

We didn't so much arrive at the swamp as stop when it got too deep even for Bubba's huge truck. He pulled over to a massive tree. When he opened the door, we were able to step straight out onto a branch that was half submerged in gooey water.

A flat-bottomed swamp boat was tied up on the other side of the branch. Bubba jumped in and reached up to give me a hand. I handed him my camera bag and jumped in and sat up front. Bubba handed me the bag and started up the motor.

"As I told you on the phone," he said, "something has been eating the gators. It's been upsetting the balance in the swamp."

"Do vampires kill gators?" I asked. The word vampire didn't seem farfetched here where trees grew out of the water and wept Spanish moss. I could hear birds calling from the branches high above. The sunlight was dyed green by leaf and moss. Other than the smell it was like being in a magical other world.

The stink got worse as we rounded a corner and I saw a dead alligator caught in the roots of a mangrove.

"Not if they have something warm blooded to kill," Bubba said, "but if they were forced to take a gator, they wouldn't eat any flesh." He pointed to where something had been gnawing at the creature's stomach. "And they wouldn't eat it from the inside."

He put the motor into neutral and grabbed an overhanging branch to bring them to a stop.

"Get your camera ready," he said, "but stay quiet."

I got out my camera and checked the batteries and card again. I took some shots of the dead gator and played with the settings until I was happy with the images. As usual when I focused on my photography I tuned out everything else. I didn't think when a frog climbed out of the water and sat on the gator. I took its picture. I took a picture of the next one too. I could zoom in close and get a sharp focus on the frog's teeth.

Part of my brain sat up and stated firmly that frogs shouldn't have teeth. It was the same part that had sent me up the ladder the day before. The rest of me kept taking photos as more frogs swarmed onto the gator and started taking bites out of it. They were eating it hollow. One of them bit into an air bubble. The air suddenly reeked of rotting flesh as the corpse made a sighing sound and sank beneath the water.

"Ugh," I said, "that's disgusting."

The frogs in the water turned to look at us. I'd seen lots of frogs over the years. They'd look at me to decide if I were a threat. These frogs were deciding if I was lunch.

"Hold on," Bubba said. He put the motor into reverse and we were speeding backwards. He pushed the tiller over and switched gears and we were going forward through the water weaving in and out of the trees. I looked over his shoulder and saw that we were only very slowly pulling ahead of the frogs.

I did what I always do in these situations. I took pictures. My card recorded image after image of frogs swimming impossibly fast and making long hops from low hanging branches. They all had the same surreal snarl that showed the sharp teeth that lined their mouths.

"When we get to the truck, get straight into the cab and buckle in. It will be a rough ride out."

I packed my camera in my bag and made sure it was secure. The bag went over my shoulder. My feet found the big branch before the boat stopped moving and I had the door open and was across the truck and buckling in as Bubba tied the boat and jumped into the truck. The frogs made it to the branch and hopped into the cab before Bubba could close the door.

A frog landed on my knee and gave me a wicked grin. I was strapped in and couldn't move. I heard cursing as Bubba swatted at the frogs on his side. He wasn't strapped yet and could reach down to grab the ones that were trying to gnaw through his boots. I reached into the camera bag and found what I needed. I thanked myself for being so anal about always keeping the bag in order. The frog jumped toward my face and I snatched it out of the air and drove the six-inch nail in my hand through its brain.

Between us we killed off the five frogs that had invaded the truck. By this time the entire truck was covered with frogs which were all trying to claw their way inside. Bubba put the truck in reverse and did a fast reverse turn. Frogs flew through the air and splashed into the water on all sides. We hit the first bump hard and sent more amphibians back where they belonged.

We drove back in silence. I held on for dear life as Bubba spun tires and got every bit of speed possible out of the truck. I couldn't see anything following us, but I was happy that he was taking no chances. We finally pulled up in the yard and Bubba shut off the motor. He picked up the bodies of the frogs where we'd thrown them behind the seats.

"I have this great recipe with white wine…"

"I don't think so," I said, "I've seen what those things eat."

"OK," he said and pushed the door open and swung down to the ground. I barely caught my breath to warn him about the frog that launched itself from the truck bed when Mars jumped up and caught the frog in his jaws. I heard the crunch as the huge dog bit down on the frog. He shook his head and sent pieces of the frog through the yard. Bubba patted him on the head and dropped the dead frogs from the truck. The dog shredded those frogs too.

When he was done, Mars bounded up into the truck bed. I looked at him through the window and he panted laughter at me. I waved back at him and climbed down the ladder as Mars checked every nook and cranny in the back. He jumped back down and landed lightly beside me. Diana came up beside me and licked my hand.

As we walked into the cabin I saw blood on Bubba's leg.

Chapter Three

"One of those things bit you," I said, "I hope they aren't poisonous."

"It's alright," Bubba said, "it must be frog blood."

"Pants off," I said and went to get his first aid kit. The dogs were sitting with their tongues out. I wasn't sure if they were laughing at me or Bubba. I turned to go back to Bubba and saw that he'd gone commando today. I focused on the oozing bite on his upper thigh.

"I couldn't go in your room and get clean clothes…" Bubba said.

I wiped the blood off his leg and he breathed in through his teeth. I couldn't help but notice that it wasn't from pain. I was about to make some offhand comment when I looked closer at the bite. It was disappearing as I looked at it.

"I can explain," Bubba said, "but can I put my pants back on first?"

"Go in your room and get what you need," I said. "I'm going to take a shower and think."

I dumped my clothes on the floor, wrapped up in a towel and went to soak. The shower ran as hot as I could take it and gradually the water and repeated applications of soap removed the smell of swamp and frog guts. What it couldn't remove was the sight of that bite healing like a time lapse movie. It played over and over in my head. OK, I'll admit that there were commercial breaks for other sights that I was sure I didn't want removed. It made for a very odd shower.

The water started losing its heat so I decided to escape before I got the cold shower I was beginning to think I needed. I wrapped up in the towel again and headed for my room. I immediately tripped over Diana and let out an undignified squeak. It wouldn't have been nearly so bad if Bubba hadn't run from the kitchen to see if I was alright. And if I hadn't dropped my towel. *Oh well, fair's fair.* I picked up the towel and made myself decent while Bubba turned beet red. Diana had that look that meant she was laughing at both of us.

I got dressed and headed for the kitchen. Bubba was trying to pretend that he wasn't still pink. The food smelled delicious. Taking my spot at the table I poured wine for both of us and smiled at him.

"Relax," I pointed at Diana, "it was her idea." She wagged her tail a little, but didn't look at all repentant. "I've spent enough time in camps and such that nudity isn't a big deal for me. Just remember I've got a six-inch nail in my camera bag."

"I've seen you use it too," Bubba said.

We ate supper while Bubba slowly became the competent, suave mystery man I'd come to expect. We were sipping a second glass of wine when I leaned back and looked at him.

"You have your pants on now," I said, "how about that explanation?"

"My name isn't really William Robert Spencer, though that's what I'm called in this time." Bubba settled oddly and I wondered if he'd ever told this story to anyone else. "It is Juan Charles de Tigre and I was with Ponce de Leon when he came to Florida in 1513. Francisco and I got separated from the rest, mostly because Francisco was more interested in gold than the Fountain of Youth.

"He didn't find any gold, but he found plenty of trouble. We came upon a tribe of natives and he decided to take a girl. I argued with him, but he was superior to me and he wasn't afraid to use the sword he carried." Bubba waved at the art in his home, "As you can see I was more interested in other things. The girl wasn't enthusiastic about the idea either. Francisco killed her, then raped her. I hit him with a club while he was occupied and tied him up. The tribe found us shortly after that. I really expected to die in that moment, and looking at that poor girl, I was ready to.

"The shaman had other ideas. He saw the girl's blood on Medea and decided that making the poor bastard drink blood for all eternity was a good punishment. They knew about the Fountain of Youth. They called it a cursed spring. The shaman mixed blood and herbs into the water and forced

Medea to drink it. He went mad. He almost broke free but the warriors pinned his hands to the ground with their spears while the shaman explained the way it was going to work.

"He was going to live off blood and only blood. Any other food or drink would make him deathly ill. It doesn't need to be human, but Francisco prefers human. He can't leave the swamp. If he tries, he just falls over.

"My punishment was to be Francisco's keeper. I make sure that he doesn't somehow escape. When he tries, I put him back. I also try to limit his depredations. The shaman made it so he couldn't prey on the innocent, but his definition of innocent is very limited. Our fates are linked. As long as he's alive, I have to be a barrier between him and the world."

"So you've been alone for five hundred years?" I asked, maybe all the wine was making me hear things. I took another sip anyway. Bubba wasn't the first I'd met who thought he was a creature of the night, just the first to heal like one.

"Not always alone," Bubba said, "but for the last hundred years it has been all but impossible to keep my secret, never mind have a relationship with someone else while doing that."

"You talked about vampires," I said, "as in more than one."

"Medea likes killing and he likes sex. He really likes to combine the two." Bubba looked down at the table. "If one of his victims bites him during the act, then they become a lesser vampire when they die. Medea ignores the other vampires. Their blood mustn't taste good to him and he has no other use for them. They make their own way and have to figure out what they are and how to live, if you call it living."

Bubba poured more wine.

"If they leave the swamp, they don't faint or get weak, so I have to stop them."

"I see." The wine looked like blood in the glass for a second and I almost gagged. Instead I sniffed it and let the heady aroma of the grapes remind me it was wine.

"Do you?" Bubba said. "The people he preys on are the people I know in town. Young girls, women, even some men - if they answer Medea's call then eventually I must put a stake through their heart and sink them in the swamp. The last one was a cheerleader from the high school. She was still wearing her uniform when she tried to rip my throat open."

I took a long sip of wine.

"Tell me about the dogs."

He laughed and in a flash turned from a somber killer of cheerleaders to an enthusiastic dog owner.

"They were Ponce de Leon's dogs. He had them bred with some idea of making himself look powerful. They were smart dogs and they didn't like Ponce de Leon. Mostly because he had no idea how to treat them. When Medea and I got lost, the dogs followed. They found us after the shaman had set me loose again. I kept them with me for company. In the early days, they used to wander off a lot. They must have found the Fountain of Youth and drank from it. Their wounds heal as fast as mine and they never age. Never had puppies either. They're the ones who let me know when the vampires leave the swamp and they track them for me."

"For some reason it is easier to believe that they are five hundred years old than to believe that you are."

Bubba laughed again.

"Time doesn't sit on them the same way. They just live each day and never count the years."

"Not a bad way to live," I said.

"Not for a dog," Bubba said, "I find it more difficult. I have to remember how old I'm supposed to be. I can change my apparent age some, so I get older until a young 'cousin' appears to take my place. That's getting harder as you need ID for almost everything now."

"I can see that would be a problem," I said, but I was still thinking about the dogs. I stood up and took Bubba's hand and pulled him to his feet. Living for the day felt like a pretty good idea right now.

"I don't think this is a good idea…"

"I'm no innocent," I said. He still held back, so I kissed him. We both tasted of fine wine, but he had a deeper, darker taste to him. The taste of years, I thought. Bubba just stood and let me kiss him. That was fun, but I wanted more. I had an idea that he did too. I ran my hand through his hair and caught a faint whiff of swamp. Was I really sure I knew what I was doing? It didn't matter because whatever rational place in my mind that might have held me back couldn't talk louder than the rest of me that didn't care.

I let my hands wander across his overalls to find the snaps that held the straps. I undid those and they fell to the floor. I looked down and saw that he was going commando again, and that there was a part of him that thought this was a marvelous idea. My hand did a little more wandering and his reserve vanished with a moan.

He started kissing me with passion and his hands were finding places to make me moan.

My last sensible thought that night was that I hoped the dogs enjoyed the show since we never made it past the couch.

Chapter Four

I woke in my bed with a warm body at my back. I rolled over to give Bubba a kiss good morning and came face to face with Diana. She licked my face and panted at me.

"Laugh at me, will you?" I said and pushed her off the bed.

I smelled coffee on the way to the shower and made a detour to the kitchen for my kiss. The kiss led to another kiss and Bubba turned the heat off under breakfast while we followed the kisses to the logical conclusion.

He finished cooking while I took my somewhat delayed shower.

"I must be more out of touch than I thought," Bubba said, "I wasn't aware that life moved this quickly these days."

"I've spent more than my fair share of time shooting pictures in war zones." I said. "I learned that if you wait for tomorrow, it may not come. Between vampires and carnivorous frogs I may not have time to waste."

"That makes sense," Bubba said, "but we do need to decide what to do with the carnivorous frogs."

"Vampires aren't a problem?"

"They are a problem," Bubba collected the dishes and started washing up, "but they are a problem that the dogs and I have managed for

98

centuries. The frogs are something new. I don't know what will happen if they get out of the swamp."

"What do we know about them?"

"You saw. They are aggressive and work in large groups. Enough of them together can kill an alligator."

"I think it only takes one to kill the alligator," I rubbed my eyes. "The gator probably swallowed a frog or two and they ate it from the inside."

"Yuck," Bubba started drying dishes. "So swallowing them whole is bad. I wondered why the dogs tore them apart. Now I know."

"Just how smart are those dogs?"

"They were smart dogs to begin with," Bubba hung the towel up and sat down at the table with me.

"After all these years I think they are at least as intelligent as I am. We are a team."

Mars bounded into the room and gave a single woof. Bubba snapped to attention.

"Trouble," he said, "a vampire is making a break from the swamp."

"I thought vampires couldn't go out in the sun?"

"That's the movies, Sally. These vampires don't like the bright light, but it won't kill them. Wait here, I'll be back in a while."

"No thanks," I said, "I'm coming with you." Bubba looked like he was going to argue, but Mars barked again and he just waved his arm. I ran and grabbed my camera bag and was climbing the ladder as Bubba fired up the truck. I swung over him into my seat and fastened in as he pulled out of the yard. Mars jumped up into the back of the truck as we turned onto the road.

Bubba steered according to the dog's directions and we soon saw Diana waiting for us. She was all business this morning. No lolling tongue or laughing eyes on her now. We followed her a little slower through the wet field, but it didn't take long for us to see the group of vampires.

They saw us about the same time and started running. They were almost faster than the truck. When they saw that they couldn't outrun us, they split up. Diana and Mars each ran full out after a vampire while we bounced through the field after a third.

It looked like a young woman. She was wearing the remnants of jeans and a shirt. Watching her it was obvious that she was no longer human. She didn't so much run as bound across the field and occasionally used her arms for extra lift or to land. I expected Bubba to stop and dispatch her, maybe with a stake through the heart or with a magic sword. What did I know?

What he did was hit her hard enough with the truck to send her cartwheeling across the ground. Then he ran over her. I felt the bumps as front and back wheels hit her. I could also hear the screams

as we headed cross country toward the last place
we saw the fourth vampire.

"Mars or Diana will finish her," Bubba said,
"we need to get to the last one before it finds
anyone."

We slashed through brush until Bubba
thought he heard screaming.

"Damn," he said, "too slow."

We burst out of the brush into a clearing
where the vampire held a little girl like a rag doll in
one hand while she gnawed at the throat of a man.
A woman lay broken in the dirt between us and the
vampire. There was a pool of blood around her
neck.

Bubba skidded the truck to a stop and
grabbed something before jumping out. The
vampire threw the man at him and spoiled the
attack. It held the girl like a shield between them.

What Bubba held was a wooden staff as long
as he was tall. It was sharpened at both ends. Every
time he moved to attack the vampire would put the
girl in the way. I saw a shorter stick with a point
behind the seat. I picked it up and climbed out of
the cab onto the hood of the truck.

Bubba and the vampire were still circling
below. I could tell that Bubba was steeling himself
to stab through the girl. I waited until the vampire
had its back to me and I jumped toward its back
with the stake held in both hands. Something must
have warned it because it spun to put the girl

between it and me. Unlike Bubba, I couldn't stop. Instead I threw the stake away and latched onto the little girl and tried to pull her away. For a split second the vampire was off balance and Bubba lunged to finish the vampire.

His spear hit the mark. It passed through the vampire's heart, scraped the little girl's ribs and passed through my gut.

I don't know whether his scream or mine was louder.

Mars and Diana ran into the clearing and skidded to a stop. Bubba pulled the spear out of me and picked me up and carried me to the truck. I was still screaming in pain, but he laid me on the tarp in the back and drove back toward his cabin.

I knew I was dying. I'd been shot on one of my assignments. This felt worse. Blood leaked out of me and took my strength with it. I watched the tree tops pass. We had just made love that morning. Would I have done anything different if I'd known?

The sky started turning dark even though the sun burned on my face. I was glad I'd met Bubba. I was sorry I didn't have more time with him. It was my only regret. Not bad, I thought, to die with just one regret. I let the dark carry me away.

Chapter Five

I always thought dying would be easier; my soul wafting away on a cloud of light or darkness and that would be it. I'd always lived as if it was what I did in this world that mattered, not the next. So it was a shock to see the warm, welcoming light that people talk about, but I saw it as if through a dirty window. I couldn't reach it. I could feel the tentacles from behind me that gripped my soul and refused to let me move on.

I have no idea how long I fought to get to that window and that light. It might be covered with filth, but I knew that window was the path to something extraordinary. The tentacles tightened their grip. They whispered of sweet life. A life that wasn't under any compulsion. I knew that if I gave into them that I would become like that woman vampire who used a child as a shield after murdering the parents. I would stay here and battle for all eternity rather than become that monster.

The darkness was a battle ground. The light beckoned silently while the tentacles whispered. I got tired of both. I turned away from the light and faced the tainted darkness. This wasn't the friendly night of the grave. It was poisonous with flashes of sickening colour in it; demanding that I worship my own desires. I like myself, but there are plenty of times that I am an iron clad bitch. The only thing that I held absolutely certain was that I was responsible for myself and that meant for not hurting other people.

I formed a sword from my will and held it fast. If the light wasn't going to claim me, it could just wait. I would deal with these effing tentacles myself. I started chopping with my sword.

I am not the most important person in the world. I am not even the most important person in my own life.

Tentacles fell to dust.

I don't have the right to take what I need from others.

More dust.

I don't need to live forever. I just need to live today.

There was only one tentacle holding me.

I love Bubba and would live or die for him, but it is time to end the swamp.

The last tentacle fell away.

I forced my eyes open and looked up into Bubba's eyes. They were filled with tears that poured down his cheeks. I tried to lift my arm to wipe them from his face, but my arm wouldn't move. I could feel it; even wiggle my fingers, but I just didn't have the strength to lift my arm.

"Is she going to be alright, Daddy?" a young girl asked as she came into the room. She was carrying a tray with tea and a plate of food on it.

"I think so sweetheart," Bubba said. He dried his eyes unselfconsciously as he picked up the tea from the tray. He looked at me and smiled as he lifted me and gave me a sip of the tea. I was suddenly ravenously hungry. I tried again to move my arm and I was able to lift it off the bed.

Mars barked from the other room and Bubba's face changed.

"Sorry, but I have to go." He touched my face like he was afraid that I would fall apart, then ran out of the room. I heard the truck roar to life and drive away.

"I'm Sherry," the girl said, "Daddy has to go kill monsters."

Sherry stayed with me and fed me toast dipped in the tea.

"Daddy told me that you got hurt when you saved me from the monster. We've been taking care of you."

"How long?" I was amazed that I could talk. I expected my voice to be raspy and weak, but it sounded normal to me.

"You've been sleeping for five years," Sherry said. "Daddy's been sad, but he'll be happy now."

"Five years?" I looked at myself. I should be wasted away, but under my nightgown my arms looked like they always had. I ran my fingers through my hair. They stuck in a braid that ran off my pillow and under the blanket.

"It's my job to braid your hair," Sherry said, "do you like it?"

"It's wonderful," I said. "What about food and…"

"We feed you every morning. You have soup at night. Daddy takes care of keeping you clean."

I marveled at the matter of fact tone in which this young girl talked about caring for me.

"So now what?" I said to myself.

"Would you like to see my kittens?" Sherry asked.

"Sure," I said and without thinking, I swung my legs to sit up in bed. "Do you know where Bubba, your Daddy, keeps my clothes?"

"Sure." Sherry pulled open a drawer and started handing me underwear and clothes. I got dressed and felt better for having clothes on. It didn't surprise her that I went from barely being able to move to walking in less than an hour.

Sherry took my hand and led me out to the back where the pig pen was. I couldn't tell if it was the same pig. The sow came over to the fence and Sherry rubbed it between the ears. She took me to a shed at the back that looked like it held firewood. There was a box with a blanket draped over it. She pulled back the blanket and I looked into the box.

"Those are cougar kittens!" I said.

"Of course," Sherry said, "they're Myrtle's." As if the name conjured up the cat, a mountain lion padded into the shed and rubbed up against Sherry like an oversized house cat. Myrtle sniffed delicately at me and licked me with a tongue like sandpaper.

Alex McGilvery

"See, she likes you." Sherry hugged the big cat and it purred loudly. "The monsters killed her Mommy, so Daddy brought her home for me."

I expected that Mars and Diana had a lot to do with the cat's training. Now I knew how Bubba could leave this young girl alone. She had a protector who was at least as deadly as the mastiffs.

"I'm hungry again, Sherry," I said as I rubbed Myrtle's head. "Let's go get something to eat."

We were in the kitchen finishing off an immense stack of pancakes when Bubba and the dogs walked in. I'd heard the truck coming from way off. My senses hadn't always been that good, but it meant I'd cooked more pancakes so Bubba would have some to eat.

Sherry giggled at her Daddy's face when he saw me cooking at the stove. Diana bounded over to lick my face. Like that day that was yesterday for me and five years ago for the world, I licked her back.

"Yuck!' Sherry said and giggled some more.

"I didn't expect to see you up," Bubba said, "I'm delighted though." He came over slower than Diana and kissed me.

"Ewww, Daddy, she just licked Diana!"

We ate the rest of the pancakes while Mars and Diana lay on the floor beside us. Sherry chattered about Myrtle's kittens and how the cougar liked me.

"Time to do your reading," Bubba said when the last pancake was gone.

"OK, Daddy," Sherry stood up and put her plate on the counter. She gave me a hug and a kiss then sat herself in a chair in the living room and was soon lost in a book that I was sure was too thick for an eight-year old.

We cleaned up the kitchen and sat at the table with fresh coffee.

"Tell me about the last five years," I said to him.

Chapter Six

"I was sure I'd killed you," Bubba said and I could see his eyes tearing up. "I got you back here and did everything I could think of to save you. Nothing worked, nothing. I begged Mars to bring you some of the water from the Fountain, but he just whined. Diana carried the little girl into the house and put her at my feet.

"Sherry saved my life. I'd have gone mad if it was just me, but I had to take care of her. She remembered the monsters and you pulling her away. So you became her hero. We washed the blood off you and put you in the bed. Somehow you didn't die, but you didn't come back either.

"Mars and Diana did all the vampire hunting for the next few months while I tried to figure out how to be a father to Sherry. She called me Daddy from the start and I loved her as much as she loved me. When I started to go out after the vampires again, one of the dogs would stay with her. One day Diana showed up with a cougar kitten and I brought it home for Sherry. She called her Myrtle and soon the big cat was following her everywhere.

"Really the rest is just more of the same. I've been homeschooling Sherry in reading and math and such. The vampires are getting worse. I have no idea where all the people are coming from. Most of the people aren't local now. It is like Medea is trying to overload me and send the vampires out into the world. Almost every day we have to track down a vampire or two."

"What about the frogs?" I said.

"The only thing that lives in the swamp now are the vampires and the frogs," Bubba said. "It is all out war in there. The frogs are ravenous and eat anything that moves. The vampires hunt them as the last source of blood left to them. I suspect that Myrtle's mother wandered in from the west and was killed by a vampire. If it was the frogs, Myrtle wouldn't have survived. The last few times out, I've seen frogs in the fields. It's only a matter of time before they escape."

"I have an idea of what made them," I said. "When I was sleeping, I was caught between whatever happens in the next life and this force that wanted me to live wholly as a creature of my desires. I wonder if perhaps a normal frog ate a vampire somehow, maybe one that had died. It wasn't enough to make them vampire frogs, but it created a creature that lived to eat. Frogs are vicious creatures at the best of times, but add in an unstoppable hunger and fangs and you have a real menace."

"I never thought of frogs as vicious," Bubba said.

"Bullfrogs have been known to eat small animals, and so have cane toads. If you give them better weapons and put them into packs, you'd get carnivorous frogs."

"So what can we do about the frogs?" Bubba said. "There are just too many of them to hunt like we do vampires."

"We get rid of the vampires first," I said. "When I was sleeping, what decided the battle was that I rejected the desires of the tainted darkness, but I also knew that it was time to finish the business that was started five hundred years ago."

"I can't kill Medea," Bubba said, "I'm not even sure that he can be killed."

"Have you ever tried?" I asked, "This thing started because you didn't stop Medea all those centuries ago. How many people have died because of him? We can't continue to just clean up after Medea. We have to go after the source of the evil."

"Remember that my fate is linked to his," Bubba said. "If he dies, so do I."

"Is it better to live because a monster kills people? I don't want you to die. I don't want to die, but I refuse to live because something else is killing people. I'd rather be dead than have the blood of all those people on my hands."

Bubba's face turned to stone and he threw his coffee cup against the wall. I watched the coffee drip down the wall as he went out the door. I heard the truck start up and the tires spin on the gravel.

Sherry climbed into my lap. I saw tears on her face and felt my own tears falling. We hugged each other and wept. I hadn't wanted to wake up to this. The dogs whined and paced in and out of the kitchen. I'd never seen them so upset.

Our tears ran out and Sherry fell asleep in my arms. I didn't know where her room was, so I laid her on the couch and covered her with a quilt. I cleaned the coffee off the wall and sat in the kitchen with Diana's head on my lap and thought.

I remembered everything that we had done in those few days during which I'd fallen in love with Bubba. I hadn't planned it. I'd come down to do an assignment and to get my photos into National Geographic. I didn't know where Bubba was, I didn't even know where my camera was. I didn't care about the camera. It had been my excuse to stay detached for far too long. I wasn't done with photography, but it wasn't going to be an escape from life any more.

The first shadow flitted across my peripheral vision and I realized two things. Bubba hadn't come home and it was dark outside. Three things, the vampires were here in force. If Bubba wasn't ready to bring the war to a conclusion, the vampires were.

"Diana, stay with Sherry," I said, "Mars, call Myrtle in. We'll need all the help we can get." I started looking for weapons. Mars returned with Myrtle and he had some stakes in his mouth. I took them from him and caressed his head.

"We guard this room and only this room," I said. "No vampire is going to get close to Sherry.

Whatever it takes, whatever it costs." Mars growled and set himself in the hall to the bedrooms. Diana crouched in the door as Myrtle took over guarding Sherry. I laid the stakes on the table and kept one in each hand.

"Come on you bloodsucking bitches," I said softly. "It's time."

My senses were on overdrive. I smelled the blood when they tore the sow apart and I heard the squeal of dying kittens. The vampires were laughing at us. They were going to destroy everything before they went after us.

The first attack came from the front door. Diana suddenly rolled on the floor with a vampire between her teeth. She shook her head and the snapping of bones accompanied the vampire's scream. It was cut off as Diana tore the creature's head off. It only took seconds, but in those seconds two other vampires entered the house. I heard Mars begin to move to attack.

"Stay," I said, "guard the hall." Glass broke and Mars focused on the hall. Sherry woke up and screamed as I attacked the two vampires in the kitchen. I expected to be striking at shadows. They were the fastest creatures I'd ever encountered. I was as astonished as they were when my first stake pinned a vampire to the floor and my second blow drove a stake through a vampire heart. Both died without a whimper. I wrenched the stake from the second vampire and picked up another one from the table.

"Get into the corner, Sherry," I said, "away from the window. Myrtle will guard you."

"Yes, Mommy," the girl said and I heard her scramble into the corner furthest from the window. That 'Mommy' that I had never expected in my life lit a fire in me. Some vampires attacked from the bedroom hall and Mars tore into them. He blocked the hall for now. More were coming in the door, but Diana stood firm and shook them like rats. The living room window shattered inward and vampires poured into the room.

I smiled and began killing, losing track of how many things I killed. The stakes ran out so I broke the legs from the kitchen table to use. Sherry continued to cry softly from the corner where Myrtle stood over her. They gave up on the attack on Mars. I heard the retreat out into the night. They left off the attack on the door as well. No more came in the window, but I was left with three. Two were big men who were as fast as I was. A tiny girl who was barely older than Sherry was the third. She had a mad grin on her face. One of the men picked her up and threw her over my head. I jumped up and speared her as she passed. Her scream meant that it wasn't a death blow.

While I was in the air the two big vampires lunged at me. The first one I stuck with the table leg and it fell back without a sound. The second one got his claws on me and tore open my side from shoulder to waist. I got my hands on his neck, but all the miraculous strength had left me. He bent his head down to tear out my throat.

I knew that Myrtle had finished off the little girl vampire. Sherry was petting the cat and whispering to it. I hoped the cougar wasn't too badly hurt. Diana and Mars weren't moving. They'd won their battle; the last vampire was too strong for me and I couldn't push him away. Now, I was going to die. That wasn't so bad, I'd died before, but it would leave Sherry at the mercy of this monster.

Bubba flew in the door and wrenched the vampire off me. He didn't bother with stakes, he broke the vampire over his knee, then tore the head off and dropped the pieces. Sherry ran to him and clutched him tight.

"I'm sorry," Bubba said, "I'm sorry, I'm sorry."

As I closed my eyes, laughter floated in from the woods.

Chapter Seven

The first thing I did when I woke was check if I'd been asleep for another five years. Sherry in the chair beside my bed still looked like the eight-year old girl I'd fought to protect. She was wearing pajamas covered with teddy bears, still asleep and I let her stay that way. From the light in the room it was late morning. It wasn't a familiar room, so I guessed that it was Sherry's.

She moaned and opened her eyes. She screamed and threw herself at me when she saw my eyes open.

"I was so afraid that you wouldn't wake up again," she said. "I wasn't afraid of the monsters. I knew that you wouldn't let them hurt me, but there were so many of them. I'm glad Daddy came back. He's fixing the windows. Diana and Mars are OK now and Myrtle is going to be fine. They killed Myrtle's kittens." Sherry's tears wet my face and I held her tight and let her cry herself out. She fell asleep in my arms so I lay there and soaked in the love and trust that this girl had for me.

I was lying in the bed holding Sherry when Bubba knocked on the door.

"Hello," he said. "I'll understand if you never want to talk to me again."

"Come here, you big lunk." He came over and sat on the bed and brushed his hand across

Sherry's hair. His dark skin looked even darker against her gold hair.

"I went out looking for Medea yesterday," Bubba said quietly. "I was so angry. I was determined to kill him and it would be your fault that I was dead. I drove all over the swamp and saw nothing but frogs. I was ranting and raving about how selfish you were while you were defending my home. I almost killed you twice." He stood up. "I'll never forgive myself." He left the room.

I laid Sherry on the bed and covered her up. Bubba was in the kitchen staring out the window. He didn't turn when I wrapped my arms around him. He didn't move when I kissed the back of his neck. I moved my hands down and unbuttoned his jeans. He groaned and started shaking. Walking around him without removing my hands I lifted my face and kissed his tear stained face. He clutched me to him and kissed me passionately. I remembered that it was just days for me since we made love, but years for him.

Bubba picked me up and carried me to our bedroom. The glass from the shattered window was gone. He dropped me on the bed and I pulled his pants down. He stepped out of them and closed the door. That gave me time to lose my nightgown. I briefly noted that there wasn't even a scar where the vampire had clawed me last night.

We loved with abandon. It was as if we were filling a yawning hole within us with the physical sensations of our love making. Finally, we were exhausted and just lay in each other's arms. I could have laid there forever, but there was a quiet knock at the door.

"I made lunch," Sherry said through the door, "I was hungry."

"We'll be out in a second," Bubba said and began putting his clothes back on. I followed suit. We walked out to the kitchen hand in hand.

"I made tuna fish sandwiches," Sherry said. We sat down and ate. Bubba refused to let go of my hand, so we ate one handed.

"So are you going to get married now?" Sherry asked.

Bubba sat there with his mouth open and I laughed.

"I'd love to get married, Sherry," I said, "but it is more complicated than just wanting to."

"Why?" she said. "Do you want to marry Daddy?"

"Yes," I said.

"Daddy," Sherry said, "do you want to marry Mommy?"

"Sure," he said, 'but…"

"So, I announce you married," Sherry said. "You can kiss, but only kiss." She made a face. "You keep the other stuff for later."

I leaned over and kissed Bubba on the lips. It was hard to kiss through the smile on my face. He had a stunned look on his face.

"But," he said.

"If Sherry says we're married," I whispered to him, "are you going to argue with her?"

"No," he said and kissed me back. "So now what?"

"You finish the sandwiches," Sherry said. "Then we have to clean this place." She put her hands on her hips. "It's a disaster."

The rest of the day and the next few days were spent putting the cabin to rights. Bubba picked up new windows and installed them. Sherry and I washed walls and painted. Bubba had dragged all the bodies into the swamp, but Sherry insisted on putting a marker up for Myrtle's kittens.

It was one of the happiest times of my life. Working beside Bubba and Sherry and sleeping beside him every night filled my heart to overflowing. I don't know what it was that kept me alive those five years, but I was thankful for this second chance. No overwhelming desire to drink blood or kill the people I loved came over me. Whatever had happened to me, I wasn't a vampire, more like Bubba, actually. I could live with that.

It wasn't all light though. Bubba built heavy shutters to go over the new windows and we closed and barred them every night. Myrtle slept in Sherry's room while Diana and Mars slept with one eye on the door.

I started dreaming of Medea a week after the battle with the vampires.

"I'm impressed that you were able to kill my slaves," he said, "but you are incomplete. Even with all your strength, you are weak. Come to me and I will complete the change. We will rule the world together."

The dreams were easy to ignore. Medea smelled of blood even in my dreams. I had no interest in his offer.

"Just push him out of your head," Bubba said, "don't let him get to you."

"We have to finish this war," I said, "I'm sure that the reason you haven't had to chase any vampires all week is that he is holding them back for another attack. Maybe he thinks that if you're gone that he will be able to leave the swamp."

"I don't know how to find him," Bubba said. "The swamp is huge and I could look for years and not find him."

"I could find him," I said.

"No," Bubba said. "I've almost lost you twice. I can't lose you a third time."

"It is only a matter of time before he is strong enough to attack again. Or what if he doesn't attack here? What if he sends ten, twenty or more vampires out of the swamp? They could kill everyone in town."

"I don't like it."

"Neither do I, but he has a weakness."

"What is that?"

"He thinks he can control me," I said, "that will let me get close enough to do some damage. You can follow me and take him by surprise while I have him occupied."

"Then what?"

"I don't need to live forever," I said, "I just need today with you."

"What about Sherry?" he said. "We can't leave her alone."

"I have an idea about that," I said.

"I'm going to come and kill monsters with you," Sherry said and waved a sharpened stick in the air.

"OK," Bubba said, "let's set it up before I come to my senses." He hugged Sherry.

The plan was simple. I would go to Medea the next time he called. Bubba would follow me. Sherry would be in the truck which was as close to a fortress as we had. If she stayed hidden the vampires wouldn't know she was there. There were a thousand things that could go wrong. I looked at Bubba and Sherry, and my love burned hot. No monster was going to threaten my family.

We had supper as usual. Bubba stocked the truck with sharpened stakes. Mars brought me a short, but wickedly sharp stake that would vanish in the sleeve of my nightgown. Sherry wouldn't move far from the stake that she'd found for herself.

The family that slays together, stays together.

Medea didn't come to my dreams that night or the next. The short stake stayed on my dresser. We put the time to good use.

The dogs patrolled through the day and we mostly slept at night. For a few days, we could pretend that we were a normal family. I seized the time and when I wasn't making love to Bubba I was seeing the world through Sherry's eyes.

Chapter Eight

"Come to me," Francisco said, "I will make you whole." He was wearing his full formal uniform and looked delicious. Bubba was big and blocky, but this man was thin and handsome. He stood in a beautiful forest in the sunlight. "Together we will live forever."

I climbed out of bed without disturbing Bubba. The big lunk was worn out from all the waiting. I quietly put my shoes on and walked out of the room. Diana looked at me as I stepped over her and I put my finger to my lips. She whined, but stayed where she was. Sherry's door was closed. I was leaving the house when I felt Mars' cold nose on my hand and he gave me a parting gift. I patted him on the head and walked toward the one who was calling me.

I could see in my vision how much he desired me and my lips curled as I anticipated the consummation of our relationship. There were lesser shadows in the night, but none of them would dare touch me. I belonged to Francisco and only him.

My feet found the path by themselves. I didn't see another living creature, not even the frogs. Everything was under Francisco's spell. With my help he would reach out from the swamp and rule the world as it should be ruled. I reached a clearing in the swamp. He was there, bathed in light. He wore no clothes at all now and he was rampant with his eagerness.

"Now, my sweet," he said, "we will finish what has been started." He bared his fangs and held out his hand. I took his hand and bared my neck to him. After all this time, this was what I was born for. He pulled me to himself and clutched my hair to push my head further to the side. It was time. I smiled in anticipation of the pain.

As he bent his head down I drove my sharpened stake between his ribs.

Medea screamed and threw me to the side. He pulled the stake out and threw it into the swamp. I rolled to my feet and pulled another stake from the sheath on my ankle. I'd been sleeping in them for the last week. Medea wasn't the only one who could play mind games.

As I shook off the last bit of Medea's control I heard the sounds of battle in the swamp. My smile had a predatory edge and I circled in toward Medea. He moved almost too fast for me to follow. I managed to put my stake between us as he lunged to tear out my throat. I'd been expecting him to try. The sharp wood scored a deep gouge under his eye.

The vampire was no longer a vision of male loveliness. His skin was old leather on bones. He looked more like a corpse than a living human, but he was still faster and deadlier than anything I'd ever met. We sparred on the rough ground of a tiny island. I knew my love and my daughter were battling for their lives close by, but I could spare no time to think of them. Whether they lived or died, they would die for certain if I lost this fight.

I feinted in and he spun to the side where I had my second stake already flashing toward his heart. As soon as he felt the point break the skin he threw himself back. He jumped high and I lifted my right hand to block, but he bounced off a branch and came in low to meet the deadly point held in my left hand.

We'd been fighting for some time when I heard a new noise. The frogs had arrived. Whatever control Medea might have had over them was gone, maybe he was distracted by my attempts to kill him. The frogs attacked both of us indiscriminately. They were appetite with no thought but satiation. I kicked them aside as I moved. Medea snatched them up and tore them in half. He drank the little blood that dripped out of their corpses. I was getting slowed up by the frogs. I had a vision of the alligator, swollen and dead, eaten from the inside. A smaller frog latched onto my hand making me drop my stake. So I snatched the frog intending to throw it away. Medea chose that moment to attack. I had a frog in one hand and my stake in the other, but I was off balance, vulnerable.

I stuffed the frog into his gaping mouth and just managed to dance away to one side. Medea tried to force the frog out of his throat, but I rammed my stake through his neck above the bulge where the frog clawed its way down to his gut. The vampire tried to scream but the most he could manage was a raspy whimper. The frogs attacked him in force and he fought them like a whirlwind.

They were attacking me as well, my strength dwindled fast. The sounds of battle were closer, but I didn't have time. The frogs were a deadlier opponent than Medea. I jumped for a low hanging branch and pulled myself up then slapped away a few frogs that were hanging on. I held on to another branch and watched the scene below.

Medea was tearing frogs apart and scattering pieces far and wide, yet no matter how many he killed there were always more. I'd never considered just how many frogs might live in a swamp this size. There was something strange happening inside Medea. His skin bulged in odd places. He'd pulled the stake out of his throat, but only made rasping grunts as he fought. The sheer weight of frogs pulled him down. A frog clawed its way into the vampire's mouth while two of its fellows were being shredded. Medea went to his knees and the frogs almost buried him. At the end Medea's lips formed a word. It might have been 'please'. The frogs burst out of his stomach and the horde poured in.

I'd watched a school of piranha attack a pig. Blood and froth covered the river and all I could see was the occasional flash of silver. This was the same. The frogs fought in a frenzy over the flesh of the vampire. In seconds, he was a skeleton with shreds of flesh hanging from his bones. Grotesquely, Medea's hands still clutched at the frogs, but now they were weak and slow. They stopped when the frogs pulled the skeleton apart in their hunger and scattered the bones across the tiny island. The skull rolled into the water with a tiny frog clawing its way in through the eye.

The frenzy done, the frogs shook themselves and hopped into the water and swam away. Soon after the last frog left, Diana bounded onto the island, followed by Mars and Myrtle. I heard the crashing of the truck approaching. It came to a halt just before the deep water that separated the island from the rest of the swamp. I dropped out of my tree and let Diana and Mars help me through the water. Bubba lifted me up into the cab. Sherry was sitting in the passenger seat. She was covered with blood and grinning from ear to ear. I lay on the floor behind the seats and let my family take me home.

I was feeling normal by morning. Sherry brought me toast and coffee on a tray and sat beside me while I ate.

"Tell me about your adventure," I said as I brushed crumbs off the bed.

"Myrtle woke me," she said, "and I climbed into the big bag like you said. Daddy carried me up into the truck and I got to ride up front. Myrtle and

Diana pretended to stay and guard the house while Mars tracked you into the swamp. Daddy drove like crazy. He ran over trees and stuff and we splashed through some really big puddles. It was fun until the monsters attacked. They were all over the truck and trying to get in, but Daddy kept hitting trees and scraping them off. Then Diana and Myrtle came and started tearing the monsters apart. We were winning until the truck got stuck. Daddy said a lot of bad words, then took his sticks and went after the monsters. He killed them like you did. Then one of the monsters climbed up and got the door open. I stuck it in the eye with my stick and it squealed and fell down. Then another one came and I stuck that one too. The last one got stuck in the door after I stabbed it, so I stuck it again and it bled all over me before Myrtle pulled it down. I got the door closed then, 'cause I'd run out of sticks. Then they were all gone and Daddy got the truck unstuck and Diana led us to you. Did you kill the boss monster?

"Yes," I said, "the boss monster is gone. The frogs ate him."

"Eww," Sherry said, "I don't like frogs."

"I don't like the ones around here either, but without them I wouldn't have been able to kill the boss monster."

"Hi there," Bubba said as he came into the room, "I was just cleaning up the truck. I think I bent an axle too."

"How are you?" I asked.

"I don't feel any different," Bubba said. "The scrapes and bruises from last night are gone." He shrugged. "Who knows? I didn't expect to be alive. Let's just take it one day at a time." Bubba leaned over and kissed me.

"Are you going to do gross stuff?"

"Yup," I said, "you'd better go and do some reading."

Sherry rolled her eyes and left the room. She made a show of making sure the door was closed.

I pulled Bubba down on the bed and we celebrated life the best way we knew how.

Chapter Nine

"Mommy," Sherry was standing at the door in her teddy bear pj's. "Can I sleep with you?"

"Sure, Honey," I said and snuggled up closer to Bubba. Sherry crawled under the blanket and latched on to me.

"Bad dreams again?" I whispered.

"Uh huh."

"Try to fill the scary places with good things."

"I try, but the monsters keep coming. I try to save the kittens, but they keep coming and my stick breaks…" She buried her head in my shoulder and I hugged her tight.

There had been no nightmares until after we'd destroyed Medea. Now she slept with us every night. Normally I would have called up one of my friends with children and they would have given me advice, but my friends probably thought I was dead. We didn't have access to the internet and we interacted as little as possible with the townspeople.

Sherry was soon asleep again, but I lay awake wondering what to do. I got an idea and fell asleep with a smile on my face. I knew Sherry would love it, but I was looking forward to explaining it to Bubba.

"I'm going to go make coffee," Sherry said as she climbed out of bed, "but I'm not putting the toast on until you get up. It got cold yesterday, adults!" I could hear her eyes rolling as she left our room and firmly closed the door.

"It's time," I whispered in Bubba's ear. He pretended not to hear me, but I had hard evidence that he was awake and interested. I kissed his neck and all my love for this man burned bright. Nibbling at his ear and running my fingernails across his stomach, just above the band of his boxers now, I heard his breathing quicken. He kicked the covers off and rolled on top of me. He kissed me back and my breathing became as fast as his. As rational thought deserted me I reminded myself to thank whoever oversaw these things for giving us a very understanding daughter.

Sherry sat at the table with a glass of orange juice and a book.

"Coffee's ready," she said and put the book down. "I'll put the toast on now." She dropped slices of her homemade bread into the toaster. Bubba poured coffee for both of us and kissed the top of Sherry's head.

"Bad dreams, Sweetheart?" Bubba said.

"I didn't mean to wake you."

"You didn't," Bubba said, "but you wouldn't believe how hard I had to work to wake your Mom."

Sherry and I shared an eye roll.

After breakfast, I helped her with the dishes.

"I have an idea about the dreams," I said.

"Mm hmm," Sherry said. She had been putting up with my ideas about the dreams for two months.

"I thought if I taught you how to fight vampires better, you'd be able to beat them."

"Really?" Her voice told me that this idea was better than the others.

"It's worth a try."

"I'll talk to Daddy about making you a sword."

"A sword?" she said. "I thought you killed vampires with stakes."

"This will be a magic sword," I said. "It's your dream, so you can have a magic sword."

"You know how to use a sword?"

"A little," I said. "I did a story in Japan about the samurai and I enjoyed the sword, so I stayed with it for a while."

"So," she said, "go talk to Daddy already."

I found Bubba in the back with the sow. He'd found a replacement, but she wasn't as friendly as the last one.

"Hey lover," I said, "I had an idea for Sherry's dreams."

"OK," he said.

"I thought I could teach her some basic sword moves. She could have a magic sword in her dreams."

"I'm a little rusty," Bubba said, "but I should be able to help."

It was surprising how quickly I forgot that Bubba was a five-hundred-year old conquistador. I drew a picture of what I wanted.

"It looks like a heavy sabre," he said. "I can cut it out of maple and laminate it so it doesn't break. I should have something for you for tomorrow."

"I'll get her started on the body positions," I said. Finding Sherry was easy. She was sitting in a chair reading a book. She put it down as soon as she saw me.

"Let's get started," she said.

"We'll go outside," I said. We went out to the front yard and I picked a space that was smooth and clear of weeds.

"So," I said, "you need to stand like this." I demonstrated with one foot back and both knees a little bent. "Keep your back straight and your weight over your hips." We worked on the foot position and back for a while. Then I had her hold her arms as if she was holding a sword with two hands. I showed her the blocks and attacks from high, low and center.

"Very good," Bubba said from the door. "I thought you'd be ready for a break and maybe wanted to see Daddy's sword." He hoisted a bundle wrapped in leather. Sherry squealed and ran to her Dad. I stretched and took a deep breath. This would be good for me. I was out of practice.

Bubba had taken Sherry back into the house, so I followed them.

The sword lay on the table. It wasn't fancy. There was no inlay, or jewels. The hilt was a simple basket. It was the deadliest thing I'd ever seen.

"May I hold it?" Sherry asked.

"Be careful," Bubba said, "it's heavier than it looks."

Sherry picked up the sword and held in with two hands like I'd shown her. She could just manage it with her small hands. I could see the sword shaking in her hands, but she tried a couple of blocks before she carefully put it down on the leather.

"Cool, Daddy."

"This is a different kind of sword than your Mom uses," Bubba picked it up one handed. He stood straight but with his knees bent, one arm behind him and whipped through a few passes. "I'm a little slow these days," he said and wrapped the blade up again and put it in the closet. "I don't want you playing with it," Bubba said, "but anytime you want to see it, just ask."

"Thanks, Daddy," Sherry hugged him, "thanks, Mom."

"We have one little bit of training left today. We can stay in here for this part." I sat cross-legged on the floor. Sherry dropped straight into the same position and looked at me eagerly. To my surprise, Bubba also sat down.

"A warrior needs to prepare themselves for battle," I said. "Your greatest weapon is up here." I tapped my temple. "If you can out think your enemy, you've won before you start." I saw Bubba nodding his head in agreement.

"Close your eyes and breathe. Feel your body, where you feel strong and where you feel weak. Feel the energy flow." Sherry sat still and breathed deeply. We'd tried some meditation as a 'cure' earlier. "Now think of a well of strength in the center of your body. Fill it with a colour that you think of as strong. Keep filling it until that colour fills your entire body. Think of it leaking out through your skin. It is making you stronger, wiser." She nodded her head and kept breathing.

We sat there in the glow of the sun together, filling ourselves with light. The light from the window was strong enough that it took me a while to notice that Sherry was glowing with a soft green light.

Chapter Ten

I must have imagined it. Sherry didn't glow again though we worked on the meditation and sword for the next month. Bubba had to make her a way to hold her wooden sword so she could wear it like a warrior.

"OK," I said holding my own wooden sword, "let's try again. It's alright to get angry but don't let your anger control you. Focus it and use it." Sherry was breathing hard and glaring at me. She'd been trying to get a touch on me all morning. We'd been practicing every day and she'd decided that it was time she was as good as me. I refused to let her get an easy touch though I slowed myself to my old speed.

"Right," Sherry said and visibly focused inward. My eyes widened as I caught a glimpse of that green glow again. Then I was fighting for my life. She came at me with everything she had, and I was hard pressed to defend myself. If it was just the speed I would have taken my lumps and been proud of her, but the first cut of her wooden sword sliced through my sword like it was butter. I dropped the hilt and put my effort into dodging. Even at full speed I felt the wind of that suddenly lethal sword pass my body. I couldn't get behind her and I was concentrating too hard to speak.

My foot caught in a rut on the ground and I fell to my back. Sherry came in to finish her opponent like I'd taught her.

"Hold!" I managed to bark. She stopped immediately and frowned at me.

"That's cheating, Mom!" she said, "I would have had you."

"You did have me," I pointed at the pieces of my sword, "but I didn't want you to hurt me in practice."

Sherry looked at the sword and dropped hers like it was hot.

"I didn't mean to," she said, "I would never hurt you!"

"I know, Sherry." I stood up and gave her a hug. "You didn't hurt me because you have discipline and stopped when I told you to." I picked up her sword and handed it to her. "I trust you with this, we'll just have to be more careful."

We picked up the pieces of my practice sword and went to show Bubba.

"I've never seen anything like it," he said, "I don't think I could cut this with the finest steel. Not clean like this at any rate." He gave Sherry a hug. "I think we'll have to work on controlling this new talent of yours."

"OK," Sherry said, "but how? I don't want to hurt you or Mom, and I don't want to chop up your beautiful swords either."

"I have some sticks in the shed that we can use," Bubba said. "If you chop them into kindling that will just save me some work.

He fetched a bundle of sticks and cut one to length with his axe.

"Let's see how you do against Daddy." He lifted the sword and Sherry attacked, but she lacked the fire and speed she showed against me.

"Sherry," I said, "I know you don't want to hurt Daddy. We trust you to control your blade. Focus so you will stop your blow before it lands."

They sparred again, but while Sherry was faster. She still wasn't focusing and there was no green glow.

"I have an idea." I said, "wait here." They downed swords and watched as I fetched some eggs from the kitchen.

I balanced the eggs on the rail of the pig pen. Sherry eyed them and twitched her sword.

"So I swing and stop before hitting the eggs?" she said.

"That's the idea. Remember how you focused when we were sparring, but now you are going to control it and be able to stop your sword in a hair's breadth."

She took a deep breath and it was like she got larger. Her sword moved faster than I could follow and then there was egg dripping down the rail.

Bubba picked up the last shell and showed it to Sherry.

"Very good," he said, "you only cut this one half-way through." He grinned and laid his stick on the fence. "Try it again. Cut the bark, but not the wood."

"Are you nuts?" Sherry said, but she stared at the stick for a long second before her sword blurred. When she came to the rest position there was a series of parallel cuts on the stick. Some were deeper than the bark, but none went all the way through.

"Cool," she said. She twirled the sword briefly then sliced clean through the top rail of the fence. "I just wanted to see if I could do it. I'll help you fix it." She handed me the sword and went off to find some wood for the repair job. I ran my finger along the 'edge' of the sword half expecting my finger to be sliced off. It was still the blunt wood practice blade that Bubba had crafted for her.

The practice sessions became a lot more interesting. When Sherry went into 'green mode' neither of us could touch her. She still worked on forms and positions, and soaked up everything that we could teach her. Her style became a blend of Spanish sabre and Japanese katana. Sherry wasn't worried in the slightest about the green glow. She was simply doing what I had told her to do, fill herself with light and push it out. Each day she came up with crazier challenges for her control, laying two pieces of paper in a stack and cut through one and not the other, or slicing through a glass bottle without it shattering. For her it was just another game.

Bubba and I talked about her abilities while she slept.

"Remember when you speared me?" I asked with my head on his shoulder. The shudder jostled me and I leaned on an elbow and brushed his hair.

"It is not something I will ever forget," Bubba said.

"The spear brushed Sherry's ribs before it hit me."

"She didn't have any injuries when Diana brought her in."

"Didn't you say that Medea was forbidden from attacking innocents?" I put my head down again. "What would vampire blood do to an innocent? I had to fight my shadows, but hers weren't deep enough to consume her yet."

"She is aging, getting older." Bubba ran his fingers through my hair.

"I don't know." I sighed as he found a knot in my shoulder and rubbed it away. "Maybe she'll keep growing until she decides to stop. Who knows, but it would explain the light and the speed."

"We'll keep watching her," Bubba said. "Whatever happens, we'll be there for her.

***

Sherry practiced her forms in the sunlit garden. She was in 'green mode' and was a blur across the yard leaving only an afterimage of her blade in the air. Then she materialized and screamed. I ran over to where she was standing, but before I reached her I saw her sword blur again. She twisted and turned like she was fighting an invisible opponent, then I got close enough to see the frogs attacking. As they jumped at her they split into two pieces and piled up on the ground.

I started snatching frogs that were further out and snapping them in half. Before Bubba made it from behind the cabin, it was over. Sherry dropped her sword and buried her face in my shirt.

"I hate frogs," she said. "I hate them."

Bubba whistled for Mars and Diana and they came running from the woods, where they'd been roaming as they usually did during the day.

"Better make a circuit and see how far these things have got," Bubba said. "If they're here, then they are getting too close to leaving the swamp." The dogs ran off as two grey streaks. "Damn," Bubba said and rubbed his eyes, "I let my guard down after Medea, and I knew the frogs were the bigger hazard.

I looked at the pile of sliced and broken frogs and had a vision of the frogs consuming Medea in their frenzy. What if that had been Sherry?

"I have an idea," I said to Bubba, "but I don't think you're going to like it."

"You'd better tell me now and get it over with then," he said. Sherry picked up her sword and put it in her belt.

"I'm ready," she said.

"We will need some carcasses, a detonator and a whole lot of explosives," I said.

"What's the part I'm not going to like?" asked Bubba.

"We're going to blow up your truck."

Chapter Eleven

We headed back to the road and off to town.

"There is something off about the town," Bubba said as he splashed through the holes that I had to winch through. Even driving my truck, he was a genius. "I'm not fond of the town, but the people have always been friendly. Last few times I went in the words were the same, but the feeling was different. Can't explain it better than that."

"If our plan works," Bubba said, "I'll let Frank know and he'll pass it along." He waved as we passed his closest neighbour, and the one who'd feel the depredations of the frogs soonest. "I think it would be best if we were just good neighbours, people are here are voracious gossipers and we might never escape if they thought we're an item."

As soon as we pulled into town, I felt the edginess that Bubba had talked about. Maybe it was not seeing anyone but Bubba and Sherry for all that time. Sherry and I headed off to pick up some supplies that we were running low on and Bubba went looking for explosives.

I was sure that the cashier was goth girl, but without her makeup and not as rail thin.

"New in town?" she asked as she rang up our purchases.

"We have a homestead out past Frank's place," I said. "We needed some staples."

"Was that Bubba driving your truck?" She bagged our groceries efficiently and I gave full credit to the town grapevine.

"We gave him a ride in. His truck needs some parts."

"Last time he came in; he took up half the parking lot." She laughed and looked five years younger. "The manager was livid until he learned how much money Bubba spent. Take care out there, ma'am. There's strange things happen near the swamp."

"Thank you," I said.

We loaded the groceries in the truck. There was lots of time before we were to meet Bubba.

"Hey," I said, "you want to get some ice cream?"

"What's ice cream?" Sherry asked.

She was on her third bowl of ice cream when Bubba walked in with another man. I didn't look at them, but I listened hard to their conversation.

"Coffee, Annie," the man said and sat himself at the counter. The woman poured two coffees as Bubba sat beside him.

"So, you're clearing some more land?" the man said.

"Yes, Bart," Bubba said, "I want to try keeping a few head of cattle."

"It'll be hard keeping them dogs from eating the cows. I bet they could eat a whole one at once. I never seen such big dogs."

"They're well trained," Bubba said, "they won't eat anything that I don't tell them to eat."

"That's good to know if I ever come to visit." Bart laughed. "So you need some dynamite to clear trees?"

"That's right."

Bart sipped at his coffee and looked to be deep in thought.

"Rightly it's against the law," he said, "but out here, who's to care? The Sheriff blew himself a nice pond out behind his house just last week. I can give you a box, but you didn't get it from me if anyone asks." He winked at Bubba. "It will be a thousand for the box. Drop by my yard in about an hour." He stood up and left a fiver on the counter. When he was gone, I relaxed muscles that I hadn't known I'd tensed.

"You don't mind if we take another hour?" Bubba asked as he sat down.

"No, I've not got anything else planned for the day," I said, "and the groceries will keep."

"We're eating ice cream!" Sherry said.

"Are you now?" Bubba said. "Do you mind if I join you?"

The next hour was one of the strangest I can remember as I pretended that I barely knew the man I slept with every night. Sherry played her part as well, chattering about shopping and ice cream and the excitement of coming to town for the first time.

When the hour was up Bubba took the truck away for a short time and came back with a tarp covering some boxes in the back. We piled in and headed for home. I could feel myself unwinding as we passed Frank's place.

"I don't remember the town being that tense when I came through before," I said as we loaded boxes into the beast.

"So you could feel it too?" Bubba asked as he passed me the last bag of groceries. He left the boxes under the tarp. I knew dynamite was pretty stable stuff, but I was glad not to be taking any chances.

"I liked the ice cream," Sherry said.

"I saw that," Bubba said and kissed her on the top of her head. "I don't know how you ate all that."

"One spoonful at a time," Sherry said and climbed up into the beast. "Let's get home, I'm hungry."

We arrived home and unloaded my truck. Sherry and I put groceries away while Bubba moved the dynamite into the beast.

When he came into the house, he carried a box with an ice cream maker. Sherry squealed and hugged him and we had to immediately make some ice cream. Fortunately, I'd bought fresh milk and cream as a treat and had it in a cooler all day. It had to set overnight, so Sherry went off to bed talking about ice cream for breakfast.

"I'll pick up the cattle tomorrow," Bubba said, "and there should be some fertilizer delivered for me as well. I'm a recluse, but some of the world leaks in. That should be a big enough boom."

"I'm sorry about the truck," I said.

"So am I, but if we'd dealt with the frogs earlier, it wouldn't have been necessary." He sighed deeply. "It's just a truck, but it is the first really modern thing I've made for myself."

"We can build another one," I said and kissed him. One thing led to another and we ended up in bed early, though we got to sleep late.

Sherry woke us in the morning with ice cream.

"I saved the kittens in my dream," she said, "I killed the monsters. Thanks, Mom." She snuggled in between us. "So when do we blow up the frogs?"

"Tomorrow if all goes well," Bubba said. "I have some things to pick up, so stay near the house until I get back."

"Where are Mars and Diana?" Sherry asked. "They should be back by now."

"I asked them to do a circuit and check on the frogs," Bubba said. "I expect they are killing frogs as they go. They don't like them anymore than you do. Myrtle is still close by."

"I think she's worried about the dogs too," Sherry said, "can I tell her to go look for them?"

"Wait until I get back, and tell her to stay out of the swamp. It's going to be dangerous even for them in there."

Bubba drove off and Sherry and I set ourselves to reading. I wasn't as voracious a reader as Sherry, but it was nice to just sit together and turn pages without worrying about vampires or frogs.

Bubba got back that afternoon and I was shocked to see that the back end was drooping down. That was a lot of fertilizer. My plan was starting to look more dangerous.

"Remember that axle I bent?" Bubba climbed out of the truck. "I'd thought I'd straightened it, but it's going again. That load is putting a lot of stress on the beast."

Wiring the explosion would be easy. We just put a detonator in the dynamite. When it went off, everything else would too. I had thought we would drive the beast in as far as we could. Push the cows onto some convenient dry land, then set the timer as soon as the frogs showed up. I figured it would take ten minutes for the mass of frogs to eat the cows, but now I wasn't sure that we could run far enough in ten minutes to get out of range of the explosion. If we set the timer longer, we ran the risk of the frogs dispersing before the blast.

In the morning Bubba wanted to leave me with Sherry, but I wanted to be there in case he needed my help. We compromised with me leaving as soon as the cows were dropped so I had a good head start on Bubba. I would wait at what we thought would be the edge of the blast for Bubba then we would both run. I knew it was a bad idea, but I couldn't bring myself to just let him go to do this alone.

We drove off after making Sherry promise to stay in the house and read. She stuffed her sword behind the cushions and very obviously made herself comfortable.

"I know you want to come," Bubba said, "but it is dangerous with the two of us."

"I know," Sherry said, "but I'm still going to eat all the ice cream and worry until you're home."

"We can make more ice cream," I said.

"But I can't make another you!" Sherry said. "I'm scared."

"I am too," I sat beside her on the couch. "But we can't let the frogs get out into the world."

"I know." Sherry turned to her book. "I'll be here when you get back."

Chapter Twelve

We drove into the swamp. Bubba nursed the bent axle and the overloaded springs. He followed the path he'd made when we had gone after Medea. If we could get near the island it would be a perfect spot for the trap.

At our slow rate of speed, it took us most of the morning to get to the island. Bubba pulled a come-along out of the space behind the seats and we set to getting the cow carcasses in position. The first one was easy, but the frogs showed up before we got the second one out. Bubba just pushed it into the water.

"Go!" he said and reached for the small box with the detonator and the timer. I took off as fast as I could through the swamp. It was easier with the trail made by the beast, but I was constantly batting away frogs. I tried to count down the minutes as I ran, but my thoughts were racing and I couldn't concentrate.

Two minutes, I thought, two minutes to set the detonator and the timer. Ten more minutes to the explosion.

The explosion caught me by surprise. I heard it, and then a crackling roar that got louder by the second. A huge hand hit me and sent me flying along with trees, water and mud. My flight stopped when I hit a tree too big for even this explosion to uproot.

I sat against the tree as the world became eerily silent. Mist and mud fell through the air, but it didn't make a sound. I was filled with a white-hot fear. Bubba. After a little while I was able to force myself to my feet. I started back toward the center of the explosion.

I couldn't walk straight, never mind run the way I wanted to. The devastation grew as I stumbled my way. Frogs were floating in the water. There were more and more as I went. Then I started seeing parts of frog. They hung from trees that had been stripped of their branches and tilted away from the blast. The ground was soupy and uneven.

I found Bubba under a tree. His face was clear of the mud, but not by much. One hand was scraping mud away.

"God," I said as I knelt beside him, "I thought you were dead."

"So did I," Bubba said, "the frogs were everywhere and I set the timer wrong. They were up on the truck, and it was either run and hope for the best or stay and get blown up."

"I'm glad you ran." I started digging at the mud. "You concentrate on breathing. I'll dig."

I don't know how long it took to dig Bubba out. My fingers and hands were raw and I'd broken countless sticks. As worried as I was about Bubba, I was frantic for Sherry. She had to have heard the blast, and she'd be waiting for us.

The sun was dropping low in the sky when we finally tumbled out of the swamp onto the road. I was as exhausted as I had ever been. I figured I'd sleep for a week when we finally made it home. Yet, beaten and sore as I was, I was satisfied that we had killed an immense number of the frogs. Farmers like Frank could set their own traps and finish the nasty creatures off.

The first we knew that we had company on the road was the headlights that shone in our eyes, blinding us for a second.

"Well," a man's voice said, "I didn't expect you to blow up the swamp with my dynamite."

"Bart," Bubba said, "what are you doing here?"

"I said that I might come out and visit," Bart said. "I found that poor girl all alone and so worried about her parents. I thought I would come and look for you."

I heard shotguns cycling a load into their chambers. Three, I thought, maybe four. Bubba tensed beside me, but I kept my hand on his arm.

"Wait," I said, barely breathing the word.

"Waiting is a good idea," Bart said. "I left some men to take care of your girl. They might do something, unfortunate, if I fail to return." He blurred for an instant and was beside us with his hand on Bubba's throat.

"Did you think with all your years of slaughter that you killed us all?" He pushed Bubba to the ground. "I didn't care until you killed Medea and I could feel death stalking me for the first time in centuries." He was back behind the lights again.

"Get in the back of the truck, and no heroics. My boys like the taste of blood and they don't really care whose it is."

We climbed into the truck and Bart drove off toward the cabin. There was another truck behind us that kept us pinned in its lights. Even if we'd had the strength, there was no escape.

The trucks pulled into our yard and the men jumped out. There were two other trucks there. I saw at least eight men plus the ones that just arrived and whatever number were guarding Sherry.

Bart kept a careful distance from us and waved us into the house.

Sherry was sitting at the table eating ice cream with a man I didn't recognize. Bart pointed to the door and the man left his bowl half eaten. Sherry jumped up and ran to hug us, then saw the pistol in Bart's hand and the two men who stepped in with shotguns. They closed the door behind them and split to cover the room. Bubba stopped her from attacking Bart.

"Easy," Bart said. "Now I'm going to have a serious talk with your parents, so I need to put you somewhere safe."

"Please don't put me in the closet, mister. I'm scared of the dark." Sherry did a credible job of the scared kid, but Bart laughed.

"I'll bet that's where Daddy keeps his shotgun." He smacked Sherry on the head. "I've read Br'er Rabbit too. Don't get any ideas, kid. We're faster and stronger than your Daddy, even before he blew himself up along with half the swamp." He pushed her against a wall next to one of the men with a shotgun.

I had to restrain Bubba again. If it were just us, I would have attacked and died fighting this monster. But Sherry was there, and I couldn't chance her getting hurt. I'd seen too many gun battles where all the wrong people got shot.

Bart pushed us to the other side of the room. He kicked Bubba's knee and sent him to the floor. He gripped my hair and put the gun against my head.

"I could feel the influence of the Fountain on her immediately," Bart said, "but I watched her eat ice cream. That means she's not tainted by Medea's curse. She's had water direct from the Fountain. Now that I'm getting older again, I want that Water." He ground the barrel of the pistol into my temple. "You are going to tell me where it is, or we are going to learn if the Water will replace her effing head. And if you're thinking that you can delay me until your dogs come back. I had some men go out with tranqs and nets. I'll breed them and have some proper dogs of my own.

"I don't know where the Fountain is," Bubba said, "I never did."

"You're lying," Bart shouted and shook me like a doll. "She's had the water. I'm going to count to three, then I blow a hole in your effing woman, then I'll start putting holes in your girlie there."

"But…" Bubba said.

Bart shot a hole in my leg and I choked off a scream.

"I have nine more shots," Bart was saying as Sherry shrieked and ran to attack him. He caught her easily and slapped her with the pistol and threw her aside. She landed on the couch and didn't move. He shot my other leg. "The next one goes into a vital organ."

Bubba roared and surged toward Bart, but he was still hurt and slow. Bart pushed me into his path and side stepped easily. Bubba lowered me to the floor and I could see the tears running down his face.

"You're weak, Bubba," Bart said and pointed his gun at us. "That's why you didn't kill Medea all those years, that's why you just hide out here and pretend to be a man. Tell me where the Fountain is and I'll let your kid live. Hell, when she's a few years older I may turn her myself. Now one more time. The Fountain. One… two…" he lifted the gun to point at my heart.

"I know where it is," Sherry said.

Bart turned to look at Sherry. Blood ran down her face from where the gun cut her. It mixed with her tears, dripping from her chin. He took a step toward her as if the blood was a magnet. He pointed the gun at her head.

"Tell me, girlie."

I screamed and lunged at him. I felt the bones in my legs grind, but it was enough to get him to move the gun. Sherry flashed brilliant green and her sword blurred. Bart's hand fell to the floor still holding the gun. He screamed but it was cut off an instant later as his body fell to the floor in three pieces. I felt Bubba push me to the floor as the men with shotguns opened fire. Pellets whistled above us. As they cycled their guns the men sighed before they too fell to the floor in pieces.

The men outside opened fire on the house, but Sherry was kneeling in front of us glowing too bright to look at. None of the bullets touched us.

I heard a roar from outside and the shooting stopped. I knew it was the sound of war dogs in full attack. I thought I heard the growl of a cougar too. The shooting started again, accompanied by screaming.

"Wait here," Sherry said and vanished in a blur. Soon after, the shooting and the screaming stopped.

Sherry came back into the cabin with Mars and Diana at one side and Myrtle on the other.

"I'm tired," she said and curled up beside us. I looked at my legs. They were still bleeding. I could feel the life running out of me. I looked at Bubba and saw that he was aging as I watched.

I hugged my husband and my daughter to me.

"I don't need forever," I said, "just today."

Holding tight to the people I loved most, I let go of life and slumped to the floor.

Chapter Thirteen

Every time I died, it was a different experience. I floated with Bubba and Sherry in my arms until I got to a clearing. It looked a little like a clearing in the swamp, only this was more welcoming.

The oldest man I've ever seen was sitting on the other side of a tiny creek that ran through the clearing. He, or maybe it was a she, was smiling and watching me. He wore woven clothes of the brightest colours. Her hair poured down her back in a silver fall.

"Excuse me," I said, "are you a man or a woman?"

"Yes," she said and he grinned toothlessly at me.

I decided that I was going to stop trying to figure what was going on. At least I still had Bubba and Sherry here.

"Where are we?"

"We are here," the elder said, "in the place between."

"Between what?"

"Life and death, desire and need, will and submission."

"Now what?"

"You choose."

"Choose what?"

"Life or death."

I looked at Bubba who had aged to be almost as old as this elder, and Sherry who slept peacefully.

"What about my family?"

"You choose."

"Don't they get to choose?"

"Would you trust them to choose for you?"

"Of course," I said.

The elder shrugged.

"What happens if I choose life?"

"You live," the elder said, "for a while longer."

"I don't want forever," I said, "just today."

"Wisdom indeed," the elder pulled a shell out from somewhere and there was smoke wafting up from it. She took an eagle feather and he fanned some smoke across the river to where I sat. I started coughing and suddenly my legs hurt.

"Thank you," I managed to say between coughs. The elder nodded her head at me and the clearing faded away. I could see two dogs running full out through the swamp. I thought they were Diana and Mars, but I was looking through a mist and I couldn't be sure. I looked down and saw myself sitting on the floor with Bubba and Sherry in my arms. Myrtle was curled up around us, but her head was up and she was staring intently at the wall.

I followed her gaze and I flew until I was over Diana and Mars as they arrived in a clearing.

It had a tiny creek running through it. It looked just like the one with the elder, only it was twisted and full of weeds and thorns. The dogs lapped up some water, then started back. I laughed to see them running with their mouth so determinedly shut, but that started me coughing again.

The coughing snapped me back to the cabin as if I were on an elastic. I was back in my body again and coughing in the smoke that was beginning to fill the cabin.

"We have to get out of here," I said to Myrtle. "Take Sherry, then come and help me with Bubba. The cougar picked up Sherry by her shirt and carried her out of the cabin. I dragged myself and Bubba toward the door. He had faded away to where he was barely heavier than Sherry. It was still hard to pull him with my legs broken by the pistol shots.

Myrtle was back and she took Bubba by the shirt and dragged him out of the cabin. I kept dragging myself. But I made a detour to the closet. Bubba's sword was the only thing he had of his old life. I pulled out the leather wrapped bundle as Myrtle took my collar in her teeth and dragged me out of the cabin.

Bubba and Sherry were barely breathing. I was doing more coughing than breathing. I watched the cabin burn. My camera was in there somewhere. I wasn't even sure where I had left it last. I didn't need it to protect me anymore. I would rather live life than photograph it.

If I stretched out my arms I could just reach my husband and my daughter. That's how I was lying when Diana bounded into the clearing and slobbered all over my face. I laughed and licked her face. My coughing stopped and I was breathing normally. My legs rearranged themselves briefly, then I could stand. Mars was over Bubba, slobbering on him, but Bubba wasn't responding.

"Take care of Sherry," I said and crawled over to Bubba. I kissed him on the lips. They were dry and cracked. It was like kissing the pages of an old book. I let my tongue dip between his lips and part them. I found his tongue and played with it. I breathed into him all the love and light that I had in me.

He moved. His lips firmed and began to kiss back. His hands came around and held me tight with the strength that was so precious and familiar. Finally, he opened his eyes and I could feel and taste the shape of his smile.

"Oh please," Sherry said, "get a room." Then she landed on top of us and the three of us wrestled and laughed in the light of our burning past.

****

I looked at the mountains through the truck window. Bubba and Sherry were oohing and aahing over them. Bubba had lived for five hundred years and never been more than a few miles from the swamp. The dogs didn't care where they were as long as they were with us and we fed them regularly. Myrtle had said goodbye and slipped back into the wilderness to find another mate and raise more kittens.

"I've never seen anything so big," Sherry said, "can we go up into them?"

"That's the plan," I said. "Up there we can build another cabin and connect with a local community. Have some real friends. It will give us some privacy, but also a place to belong."

"I don't want to be a recluse anymore," Bubba said, though we'd decided to start calling him Bill. "I didn't know the people in the town back home well enough to know something was wrong." He looked at the front page of the paper. Even from five states away the headlines screamed about human trafficking and the bloody battle between rival gangs. As overblown as the headline was it made more sense than vampires.

"Don't worry," I said, "we'll figure it all out."

"But we have so much to do," Sherry said. "Find a home, build a cabin. I have no idea how to make friends!"

"That's alright," I said looking at the light on the mountains. It reminded me of the welcoming light in that clearing. "We'll take it one day at a time. Something tells me that we'll have plenty of time to learn."

Alex McGilvery

The Thing in the Hall

The Thing in the Hall

Wolf walked through the wasteland that used to be the downtown. Like an ancient willow the city looked healthy from the outside, but its heart decayed. Wolf felt eyes on his back. He didn't slow his pace or turn his head, but his ears sorted out the sounds around him. Three sets of footsteps paralleled his course. They were uneven, uncertain; no risk to him.

Wolf came to a spot where the road widened. People scurried away from him. He stopped and turned around. He spotted two of his followers immediately, young and nervous, hands on their guns. Dangerous because they might make a mistake and squeeze a trigger a little too tightly. Wolf held his empty hands away from his side and waited. The boys relaxed and let their hands move away from their weapons. The footsteps of the last one stopped a little way behind him.

"I've come to see Rolph," Wolf said.

"Have you now?" the man behind him said, "and who would you be, to be seeing Rolph?"

"I'm Wolf," Wolf turned slowly with his hands still held away from his side. "I hear that Rolph has a problem that needs fixing."

"What makes you think he needs your help with the fixing?" The man hadn't unholstered his gun. The lines and scars on his face suggested he'd learned wisdom the hard way.

"How many have you lost," Wolf asked, "that you must arm children and set them to guarding your territory?"

"I'm no child!" a voice shouted behind him, the break in the voice betrayed the boy's fear.

"Easy, Mark," said the man facing Wolf, "I'm Ed," he continued. "You want to meet with Rolph, it's your funeral." He turned and walked away. Wolf followed.

"I could kill you right here," Mark said. His gun poked into Wolf's ribs.

"You could," Wolf said, "but a man would not. He would realize how it would humiliate his boss." The gun retreated, but not very far. It didn't bother him. Wolf had lived on the edge of death for too long for him to worry much about details, like at whose hands he would die.

Ed led them into a derelict building and along a reeking, decrepit corridor. They exited through into another square. The first electric lights since he'd entered this territory shone from an old hotel. Glass remained in some of the windows. Ed led him through the revolving door, its panels filled with boards so he couldn't see into the lobby. Clever, it would slow any attacker down enough to kill them easily.

Mark clicked the safety on his gun as he stepped through the door. Wolf looked in a mirror hung on the wall and saw that the other follower wasn't a boy as he had first thought, but a young woman. She let her gun drop so it hung on its strap. Her look made Wolf nervous. He could deal with death and guns without a thought, but that smoldering look in a woman's eyes only meant trouble. Gwythin looking at him like that got him run out of the Gats. His Chief hadn't liked that his woman still desired Wolf.

He followed Ed through a set of double doors into a large ballroom. The chandeliers were ablaze with light. Sconces set into the walls pushed the shadows back. Mark stayed behind him while the girl vanished into the crowd.

"Impressive, isn't it?" Ed said. Wolf paused and took a long look around. He saw bullet holes in the walls and stains under the feet of the men and women who stared at him with a mix of curiosity and hunger. A deep breath brought the scent of blood and fear. He didn't reply, but he nodded noncommittally. These people were ripe for a hero. Being a hero got people killed. Wolf didn't want the job, but how else could he test himself?

Ed shrugged and led him through the crowd to the far end where a big man lounged on what was once an elegant chair playing with a cup. A smaller man stood behind with the only unholstered weapon in the room. His frown was the reverse of the big man's smile.

"So, Wolf, do you come to spy us out for your old man?" The man in the chair said.

"If you know that I am Wolf, you also know that my old man has a price on my head."

"Right, something about him taking your girl for his own."

Wolf shrugged.

"So, why are you here?" the man behind the chair asked. His weapon pointed at the ceiling, but he was the deadliest man in the room. He watched Wolf with hard eyes. Wolf had heard stories of Igor's battles.

"I heard you have a small problem with your new digs," Wolf looked around the room, "I was bored and thought I would drop in and check it out."

The man in the chair laughed and waved to his right. The young woman who had looked at Wolf with such burning need sauntered over to sit on the arm.

"So, Cherry," Rolph said, "What do you think?"

"It could be … interesting," she said and looked at Wolf again. "Let him stick around for a while, Dad." She winked at Wolf while Mark behind him ground his teeth. The minx knew it too and her smile made Wolf want to leap out a window and flee into the night.

"Very well," Rolph said, "Mark, show our guest to a room. Make sure he is comfortable." Wolf fought to keep his face straight as Cherry glared at her old man.

"Lead on warrior," Wolf said to Mark. The young man unconsciously straightened under the compliment. Mark led him to a staircase. He nodded at the two men who lounged on the steps playing cards. Wolf noted that their guns weren't far from their hands. They went up three floors before Mark pushed through to lead him down a dingy hall. There was no power here. They stopped in front of a door. Mark pushed it open.

"The locks don't work, but there's a bolt for when you're sleeping," Mark said. "I sleep across the hall if you need something." He stood glaring at Wolf like he regretted not shooting him while he had the chance. Wolf sighed and dropped his gear on the bed.

"I have no interest in Cherry,"

"Don't tell her that," Mark said bitterly, "that'll just encourage her."

Wolf laughed and nodded.

"I'll keep that in mind," Wolf said, "Tell me about the trouble."

Mark turned away, but not before Wolf saw him go pale. Wolf waited for the young man to compose himself.

"We moved in last month. There's solar on the roof. Enough for lights, but not enough for hot water. It's the best digs we've ever had. A week after we moved in something came through a window. It killed three men in as many seconds, then fled before we fired a shot."

"The Weeds?"

"That's what the Chief's right hand man, Igor, thinks. He wants to lead a posse against the Weeds. Rolph won't let him. It's like he's afraid of something more than the Weeds. We've been hit once or twice a week since then. We've shot the thing, but it made no difference. They just bounce off. It only kills three men at a time, or we'd all be dead."

Wolf looked at Mark. The boy was hiding his fear well.

"OK," he said, "let's get back down to the hall."

"The thing is going to come tonight," Mark said.

"That's why I'm here," Wolf said. "I'd hate to come all this way only to miss it."

"Aren't you afraid?"

"Everyone dies," Wolf said and shrugged.

They walked back into the ballroom and Wolf could see that they'd interrupted an argument between Rolph and Igor. Cherry lounged on the arm looking bored. She rolled her eyes at Wolf. Wolf was careful to keep his face deadpan, but he could feel the heat of Mark's desire for the girl.

Rolph and Igor both stopped their talking and glared at Wolf. Igor clearly still thought Wolf was a threat. The gun was holstered now but his hand never strayed farfrom the weapon. Rolph as Chief couldn't show fear, but Wolf smelled it on him. He didn't think it was him Rolph feared. Cherry looked at him and licked her lips, but for a second Wolf saw past the mask, she too was terrified.

"Well, Wolf," Rolph called, "come and join the party. Eat, drink, tonight you are my guest."

Wolf nodded and let Mark lead him to a table that had food and bottles of liquor and beer scattered along its length. He filled a plate and took a bottle of beer then sat at a table and starting eating.

"You were at the fight between the Weeds and the Gats," the man beside him said. "Heard it was vicious."

"Bad enough," Wolf said. "We lost a lot of good men on both sides. It didn't change anything."

"The Weeds haven't attacked you since. That's a change, ain't it?"

"They're just waiting," Wolf said. "They can afford to wait."

"Huh," the man said, "I hate waiting."

"That's why you're eating here and he's sitting in that chair," Wolf said.

"Ain't that the truth."

The conversation in the room was muted and nervous as the people ate. What would terrify hardened warriors so they acted like brash youth? A fight broke out on the other side of the room and was quickly broken up. The women left as they finished eating instead of staying with their men.

"All right," Igor said when it was mostly drinking instead of eating. "Any women who haven't left, clear out. Men, even numbers to your rooms. Odd numbers, make sure you stay sharp."

"I'll stay," Wolf said, "I'm curious about this Thing that is shedding blood in your own digs without reprisal."

"I'll stay with him," Mark said.

Rolph nodded and pointed to one of the men who were trying not to look too eager to get out of the room.

"Escort Cherry to her room and stand guard outside her door." Wolf wondered if he imagined the slight emphasis on the 'outside'. He didn't think so from the baleful look the girl was giving Rolph.

The chandeliers went out. Only the wall sconces provided light. Without the main lights, there were dark shadows everywhere.

"The batteries don't have enough juice to light the room properly through the night so we turn the main lights off," Mark said.

Wolf concentrated on staying relaxed. He had no idea what was going to happen, but rumours of an unkillable creature had drawn him here to test himself against it. What else did he have to do with his life with no gang and no chief to claim his loyalty?

Time dragged on. Men who had been hyper-alert were losing their edge. Heads nodded as guns were placed on the tables or in holsters. Others who had been drinking were lying on or under the tables.

A crash came from the depths of one shadow; a scream and a brief burst of gunfire. Wolf looked over but couldn't see anything. Another scream from a different part of the room meant that either this thing was insanely fast, or there was more than one. Men turned in circles with their guns held with whitened knuckles. Wolf knew he was in as much danger from their bullets as the thing. He saw a shadow in a shadow and jumped on the table to run and leap, not into the shadow, but to where it might be moving.

He felt cold skin under his fingers. Whatever this was, he didn't think it was human. It was faster than he had imagined. It spun so fast that he almost lost his grip. He held on tight even as he felt claws ripping at his ribs. There was a burst of gunfire almost beside his head, and the Thing paused for a second.

In that second Wolf grabbed the thing's arm and heaved and twisted. There was a snap and a ripping sound, then a howl sent the men in the hall to their knees. Wolf was left holding an arm. He looked at it, then over to Mark, whose gun was still smoking.

"Well, warrior," Wolf said, "we know two things. It isn't human, and it isn't invincible."

They fired up the lights and Wolf looked around. Two huddles of men gathered around what he knew were the corpses of their fellows.

"Well," Igor said as he came from the other side of the room, "we lost two good men, and what did you accomplish?"

"It's hurt," Wolf said and tossed the arm on a table. It was already beginning to stink. Some of the warriors stepped closer to peer at it, others stepped back. The arm was grey green, and the blood that dripped from the torn end was not quite the right red. It hissed as it hit the stone floor. The muscles under the skin weren't shaped right. One warrior, braver or more foolish than the others poked at it with a finger. He pulled it back with a curse and put his finger in his mouth. He screamed and his back arched until bones cracked. He fell twitching to the floor; seconds after that he was dead.

"Water," shouted Igor. Men ran to the barrels at the side of the hall and brought back jugs of water. Wolf carefully sluiced the blood from his arms. The blood was already eating into the thick leather sleeves he wore from wrist to elbow. His clothes were a ruin. He let them fall to the floor. He sluiced his hands and legs until he was sure that none of the creature's blood still touched him.

"I come down to help the wounded and find a warrior taking a bath," Cherry's voice wafted across the room from the stairwell. "How curious."

174

"You should not be here," Igor said, "it is not safe."

"The Thing has been and gone," she said, "I'm sure the danger is over." She sauntered through the men until she saw the arm on the table. She reached a hand out to touch it. Wolf grabbed her and pulled her back.

"It's blood is poisonous," he said.

"And how would you know?" Cherry said as she yanked her arm away from him.

Wolf just pointed to the dead man on the floor.

"Cover him up," Cherry said, then walked away across the room.

"It's death to lay a hand on Rolph's daughter," Igor said.

"I'm sure he would much rather she died in agony like that poor fool," Wolf said. "If he is going to punish me for saving her life, then he isn't half the man I thought he was."

Mark handed Wolf his shirt. The younger man's shirt was skin tight on Wolf, but it was better than standing in his skin with Rolph's daughter on the prowl.

"I hear that you wounded the Thing," Rolph said from the chair at the head of the room. Wolf wondered how long he'd been there.

"So you see," Wolf said and pointed at the arm. It was little more than a reeking puddle on the table.

"An arm is small exchange for three men," Rolph said.

"It is wounded," Wolf said. "In the morning I will track it to its lair."

"Alone?"

"Send Mark and Igor with me," Wolf said. "One to watch me, and one to watch my back."

"Very well," Rolph said. He pointed to the table. "Put that mess outside, carefully. I don't want any holes in the carpet."

Mark guided Wolf up to his room and left him there. Wolf checked and cleaned his gun, then climbed into bed. After a minute, he got up and wedged a chair under the handle of the door. A few minutes later a quiet knocking at the door broke the silence. It grew louder, then Wolf heard what he was sure was a feminine huff, then silence again. He smiled to himself in the darkness and went to sleep.

****

Wolf checked the gear Mark brought him. He wore the leather sleeves on top of his shirt and had a leather breastplate as well. It didn't fit quite right and chaffed already. He ignored the discomfort. Mark fussed with his breastplate and sleeves trying to find a more comfortable way to fasten them. Igor stood like a statue.

"No guns," Wolf said, "we already know they do little good against the Thing. Keep your knives handy." He'd already left his guns on his bed, but he carried every knife he owned. They walked down the stairs and out a side door.

"Let's go," Wolf said and started around the old hotel. He expected to find a clear blood trail. He wasn't disappointed. The blood had seared into the concrete.

"This way." Wolf led off. Mark finally quit fussing and fell in behind Wolf a few steps to the right. Igor was barely audible back further and to the left. They followed the blood through the morning. As Wolf expected, it got harder to find the blood. The Thing had to either stop the bleeding or die. They didn't see a body or a pile of acid like the arm left. It was out there and hurt. *Angry too, he'd be angry if someone took his arm.*

***

The day grew warmer, and Wolf felt the heat reflected off of broken buildings and the remnants of the black road. The smell grew stronger too. Rotting concrete, rotting other things too, he figured. They heard scuttling noises a few times, mostly rats.

A loud clattering up ahead put Wolf on alert. He gave hand signals to Mark and Igor. He didn't bother to check if they obeyed. Either they would or they wouldn't, it wasn't worth turning his back on a potential enemy.

Wolf glided through the broken city. Nothing human would hear his footsteps. Years of training had made silence second nature. Neither of the others made a sound. He peered around the corner to see an old woman turning rocks over with her long stick. A rat ran, and the stick pinned it to the ground. The woman picked it up and stuffed it into a sack.

"Hey, old woman," Mark stepped out from a pile of rubble. The long stick flashed at him, and he jumped back. The woman continued her attack while Mark dodged and ran around her. Her white hair swayed and flowed like snakes as she chased the young man.

"You aren't taking them," she shouted, "they're mine!"

Wolf watched for a while, but Mark tripped on a stone and fell hard. He blocked the stick with his arms, but didn't have time to get back to his feet. Wolf ran across the street. The woman spun just as he was in range and stabbed at him with her stick. Wolf didn't dodge; instead he deflected the blow and stepped toward the woman. He trapped her hands on the stick with his and twisted until he was behind her.

"Easy," he said, "we aren't after your food." She fought his grip for a few seconds, then went limp. He held her gently but didn't let her go. She was thin, and light as a feather. He heard Mark scrambling to his feet. He also heard Igor's laughter. When Mark was out of range, Wolf let the old woman go. She spun to strike him with her stick, but Wolf was faster and stayed behind her until he could leap out of range.

"The day isn't completely wasted," Igor said as he approached, "we can sing tonight about how you defeated an old woman."

"Laugh," the old woman said. "Go ahead and laugh, Frida knows what you hunt. I've heard it skulking through the shadows." She leaned on her stick and tilted her head. Wolf realized that she was blind. "You will find it in its lair by the swamp, but you'd be better to turn back. Death stalks those waters."

"Death stalks us all," Wolf said.

"You," the woman said, "you will get what your heart desires only after death has stilled it."

"Are you a witch to tell our fortune?" Igor said. It was the first time Wolf had heard anything but absolute confidence in the man's voice.

"Right hand man to the boss of the Duns," the old woman said. "Will he still need you if you have no right hand?"

Igor's hand went to his knife at his belt, but Wolf signed him to be still.

"Silent one," the woman said, "do you have no words for an old woman?"

"If I could use a stick half as well as you, grandmother," Mark said. "I'd be a great warrior."

She laughed. Wolf expected a witch's cackle, but her laugh was rich and musical.

"You will never be a great warrior," she said, "but you will be a great man." She pointed with her stick. "The swamp lies that way. You are almost upon it." She continued to laugh to herself as she walked away from them.

Wolf smelled the swamp before he saw it. It reeked of death; a perfect place for the Thing to have its lair.

"We have to go in there?" Mark asked.

"Afraid to get your feet wet?" Igor said, but he didn't step any closer to the water than Mark. Wolf ignored them both. The swamp stretched as far as he could see through the ruins. Rubble islands poked up through the slimy water. Some even had trees growing on them. It didn't look healthy, the weeds that crowded the water looked more yellow than green. He didn't hear frogs or the call of birds.

"We'll head north along the shore," Wolf said.

"Why north?" Mark said.

"Because the last sign I saw was north of us," Wolf said. He set out along the edge of the swamp. "Be careful, the margins may not be stable. This is not a place to go swimming."

"Have you been here before?" Igor said.

"On the far side," Wolf said, "I was much younger. There are monsters that hide in the shallows."

"Monsters?" Mark said, "What do they eat?"

"Anything careless," Wolf said.

They walked north while the sun dropped lower over the swamp. They would be walking back through the dark. He was about to call a halt when he saw a patch of blood on some concrete. The Thing must have waited some time there for something. Wolf considered what would make the Thing cautious enough to wait that long before moving on.

"Back!" Wolf shouted and bounded up onto the block of cement. He was almost fast enough. Mark wasn't close to the water and leapt backwards as soon as he heard Wolf. Igor stood right on the verge peering at something further along the shore. His head came up when Wolf called, but he didn't move. In that second, a monster lunged from the depths and snapped its jaws tight on Igor's arm. He had a second to yell, then the monster pulled him into the water.

Wolf jumped down and ran to the water's edge. Mark soared past him in a dive with his knife already out. Wolf wondered how he knew he'd hit the monster, not Igor. The swamp erupted into roiling water as the monster surfaced. Mark's knife was buried deep in the creature's side. It thrashed and roared, but Wolf couldn't see either Mark or Igor.

He didn't look forward to returning to Rolph without either of them. Then Mark's hand gripped the edge of the pavement. Wolf took hold of the hand and hoisted Mark and then Igor out of the water. Igor's arm below the elbow was gone. Wolf tied a cloth tightly around the end. Igor opened his eyes as Wolf was done. He looked out at the water where the creature's thrashing gradually slowed.

"You left your knife in the beast," Igor said to Mark.

"It was stuck," Mark said and turned red, "I couldn't save both you and the knife."

"The witch was right," Igor said, "you'll never be a great warrior if you can't take better care of your weapons." He smiled weakly, "but you are one hell of a man." He closed his eyes and sagged against Wolf.

"We have to get him back," Wolf said, "we'll carry him between us." He broke off a couple of straight branches and fit them through the sleeves of his shirt. Mark did the same at the other end. It wasn't going to be comfortable, but it would do.

Wolf headed off in a straight line to the hotel.

"We're going to cut awfully close to the Weeds' turf." Mark said.

"We don't have time to go around," Wolf said. "If we get stopped, let me do the talking."

They walked steadily with few breaks, though Wolf knew Mark's arms must be burning as much as his. Full dark came when they were closest to the Weeds. The confident footsteps of men on their own turf echoed through the night.

"Men coming," he said quietly. "We put Igor down when we see them, but remember let me do the talking."

They came to an open space on the road.

"Here," Wolf said in his normal tone, "we'll put him down and rest."

Seconds later the clatter of rubble announced the other men's approach.

"Hey, so what have we here?" the first one said as he stepped out into the moonlight. Wolf heard the rush of torches being lit and flames added warmth to the cold white light of the moon. The leader was taller than him, but had no scars on either face or arm, a younger warrior sent out on patrol.

"Some Duns who've lost their way," another said. "One of them's hurt."

"Hurt, dead, it will be all the same soon enough," the first one said. "So what made you think you could trespass on Weed turf?"

"I'm not Dun," Wolf said.

"Why should that matter to me?"

"My name is Wolf," he said and stepped further into the torchlight.

"You think that we can't kill you?" The Weed stepped forward to challenge Wolf.

"Wrong question," Wolf said. "The question you should be asking is how many of you are going to die trying."

The Weed stepped back again and realized what he'd done, but it was too late. He either attacked and died, or left with what little dignity he had remaining.

"Weeds don't kill old men and cripples," he said and turned away. The torches were doused, and Wolf heard the running feet of the retreating squad.

He walked back to Mark and Igor.

"Let's get back," he said. They hoisted the stretcher and continued on their way. The moon behind ruined buildings before they were challenged by a Dun patrol. The Duns took over the stretcher and half guided, half guarded the three the rest of the way to the hotel.

A runner went to fetch Rolph as Igor was carried into the hall. Wolf had them put the stretcher on the table closest to the dais. Rolph ran in as Wolf was checking the bandage. Not much blood, but the stump was turning black.

"Another warrior gone," Rolph said, "and what do I have to show for it?"

"Not his fault," Igor reached up with his left hand to grip Rolph's arm. "Careless, swamp monster got me." He smiled and let go of Rolph. "Mark killed the monster and saved me."

Rolph looked at Mark.

"Killed a swamp monster?" he said, "Did you bring me its head?"

"No," Mark said, "it was a choice between the monster and Igor. I brought you Igor."

"Good man," Rolph said and turned back to Igor. Cherry ran in with a bag and gasped when she saw Igor. She visibly calmed herself before she stepped up and moved her father aside.

"Let me see," she said and unwound Igor's bandage. She nodded absently to herself then pulled some things from the bag. "This is going to hurt, a lot," she said, "so if you plan to pass out, now's a good time."

She gripped the arm above where it had turned dark and massaged the arm until it oozed a stinking black liquid, then squeezed it again and again until it began bleeding red. "I need whisky," she said. Someone put a bowl beside her. She ran some thread through the whisky and threaded a needle, then put needle and thread in the bowl. Cherry took a knife and splashed it with whisky before cutting away the ragged ends of flesh hanging from Igor's arm. Powder from her bag dusted the cleaned end of the arm before she used the needle and thread to sew the wound closed. She ran her hand across Igor's forehead before putting everything back in the bag.

Wolf looked a Cherry, and for a brief instant he saw a very different person than the spoiled girl he'd first met.

"Are you going to tell me that a girl has no place here?" she said.

"I couldn't do what you did," Wolf said, "you belong here more than I."

She gave him a strange look, then walked away still carrying the bag.

"Here's as good as a place as any for him to rest," Rolph said. He pointed to a few of the men. "You will stand guard with me tonight. Wolf, Mark, go rest. We will speak in the morning."

***

Wolf got out of bed while it was still dark. The sentry at the door to the hall grunted when Wolf walked past. Cherry met him in the foyer.

"Leaving already?" she asked, caught somewhere between the coquettish girl and the briskly competent healer.

"I'll be back," Wolf said, "I want no more people to die because of this Thing"

"And if you don't come back?"

"Then I will be dead."

"Is this all you want?" Cherry asked, "to kill things and prove that you are stronger than everyone else?"

"No," Wolf said, "It isn't what I want, but it is what I am." He left the hotel and found Mark waiting for him.

"I figured you would head out alone," Mark said, "I didn't figure to let you."

"Everyone choose their own death," Wolf looked at Mark and shrugged, then led the way toward the swamp.

He followed a line between their path the day
before and their way home. He wasn't sure whether
he hoped to see the old woman again, but they saw
nothing but rats and birds. The sun wasn't at its
zenith when they reached the place of the battle
with the monster. The water was flat.

"If you want to fetch the monster's head,"
Wolf said, "I'll wait for you."

"I don't need it," Mark said, "I've found who I
am." Wolf looked at him and barely recognized the
scared boy who had escorted him in to the hotel.
He nodded and walked north and pointed at the
opening of a sewer. Once there was a steel grate
across the mouth, but all that was left was a single
rusty hinge.

"That's what Igor was looking at. We have
to walk along the shore to reach it. The Thing
waited until it knew the monster was gone."

They picked their way to the opening of the
sewer. It would be shoulder height on Wolf.

"Wait here," Wolf said. "If I don't come out,
go home and bring a squad of men here."

"You think you're worth a squad of men?"

"At least," Wolf said and jumped to the
opening. He drew a long knife and headed into the
sewer.

Wolf had expected the sewer to smell, what
he wasn't prepared for was the miasma of death
that hung in the air. It made the hair on the back of

his neck stand up. It was more than just the reek of blood or the smell of rotting flesh. They were there, but underneath was something that Wolf couldn't place that screamed 'Death!' He checked his weapons and crept into the dark. He and death were old friends.

The grey light from the mouth of the sewer was enough to show him the piles of bones on either side of the tunnel. They'd been broken and gnawed. Skulls had been smashed open to give access to brains. Wolf wondered how long the Thing had lived here, and what made it suddenly start attacking Rolph's hall.

The bones stopped at a large space with three tunnels feeding into it. There was just the merest trickle of water from the tunnel on the right, but it fed a pool in the center of the space. Light filtered down from a grate set in the ceiling. The water must run away underground since the sewer Wolf walked was humid but not wet. In the weak light, Wolf saw what he thought was the mark from the Thing's acidic blood.

He walked around the fringe of the pool to the left-hand tunnel. The mark suggested that the Thing had crawled into the tunnel. Wolf peered into it. The air was still as a grave. Water dripped behind him. He spun and drew his blade.

The Thing stood knee deep in the pool of water. It looked even more alien than the arm had suggested. Its left arm held a weapon shaped like the knife that Wolf held, but larger. It was bright green like the plastic toys that still survived in places. Stuff that might have been clothes or perhaps scales covered its torso. Where the right arm had been was a tiny bud, as if the arm was growing back. As long as it took its time. The face was the worst, eyes like a fly's were set wide apart. There were no other features aside from the slitted mouth that opened to show sharp teeth.

"Time to die," Wolf said. He didn't know if he spoke to himself or to the Thing. It didn't matter.

The Thing screeched at him and leaped from the water. Even knowing how fast it could move, Wolf underestimated it and almost died in the first seconds of the battle. The green blade sliced through his leather armour like it wasn't there and he felt the burn of what would be his newest scar if he lived through the next few minutes.

Wolf slid to his left and ran his own blade across the stomach of the Thing. He felt the scrape in his teeth, but it didn't leave a mark on the Thing. He kept retreating and watched for the Thing's next move. It jumped high and bounced off the wall to come at Wolf from above. Wolf rolled beneath it and blocked the green blade with his knife notching the steel. The knife was going to break the next time Wolf used it. Instead, he threw it at the Thing and drew another. The Thing slapped the thrown blade, and the pieces fell into the pool.

The fight fell into a pattern. The Thing would lunge with shocking quickness, or leap high to attack from above. Wolf couldn't make a scratch on the Thing, but his armour hung off him like rags. He was down to his last knife. Every other weapon he'd brought was shattered. He didn't hold out much hope for this one either, but he'd learned the Thing moved its feet differently for a lunge rather than one of its prodigious jumps.

He waited.

The Thing lunged at him, and Wolf moved like he had so many times already. He held his knife up as if he were going to parry yet again. At the last instant, he dropped the knife and gripped the Thing's arm at the wrist. Wolf twisted and spun the creature into the wall. The arm snapped and the green blade came free. Wolf caught it with his left hand and whirled it through a circle that ended in the Thing's neck. He dove backward and rolled away from the fountain of deadly blood. The Thing's head rolled on the floor as the body sank into the pool. Wolf skewered the head with the blade he held and kept the dripping well away from his body.

Mark waited outside for him. Holding a knife, but where he could get away to bring help if needed.

"I heard the Thing," he said, "but I knew you would prevail."

"You knew more than I," Wolf said. "Let's get this thing back to Rolph before it dissolves."

There wasn't much of the head left when they got to the hall, but no one argued that it was anything other than the Thing. Wolf left it outside to hiss and melt on the cement.

Rolph was fascinated by the blade.

"I've never seen the like," he said. "It doesn't look or feel like steel, yet it cuts better than my finest blade."

"It cut through every knife I owned," Wolf said, "I have yet to figure out how to carry it without cutting myself to pieces." He looked at Rolph, but the man made no attempt to claim the blade.

After talking with Rolph, Wolf went to check on Igor, still with green blade in hand.

"Curious," Igor said as he peered at the blade, "tell me of the battle."

Wolf described the fight and realized something as he did so.

"The Thing was not a warrior," he said. "It was fast and deadly, but it's attacks fell into a pattern, and I was able to use that to defeat it. There were bones that looked months or even years old. I don't know why it would suddenly start attacking your hall."

"That is a tale that my father will have to tell you," Cherry said as she came into the room. She walked to Igor and brushed her hand across his forehead. Igor's hand came up to briefly hold hers. Wolf left them and went back to his room.

He returned to his room and left the blade on the table. He lay on his bed and tried to think through the puzzle, but weariness overcame him and he fell asleep.

Wolf's dreams were troubled. He walked into his Chief's hall and saw Gwythin standing with the Chief. They were looking at something with their backs to him. At the sound of his boots on the stone floor, the Chief turned and looked at Wolf with the Thing's eyes. At his touch, Gwythin also turned, and she smiled as she always did when she saw Wolf, but this time it was with the Thing's mouth.

"Come," she said. "Be the first to meet the heir to our Chief." She lifted something out of the cradle behind her and showed it to Wolf. It was a grey egg.

Wolf bolted upright in his bed, but a cool hand pushed him back down on the mattress.

"You're fevered," Cherry said. "You should have told me you were wounded. Mark brought me when you wouldn't wake." She peeled the tatters of his shirt off and dusted powder in his wounds before sewing them up. She gave him a cup with water and a faint smell of herbs. Wolf drank it down and let the cup fall to the floor.

This time no dreams troubled his sleep.
**

Wolf woke and went downstairs to find some food. He was shocked at how weak he'd become. It was the middle of the day and most of the tables were empty. He went and sat beside Mark.

"I hope you don't mind," Mark said, "but when you wouldn't wake, I was worried that you had some poison from the Thing in you."

"It never occurred to me," Wolf said, "that I might need a healer." He peered beneath his shirt. "She has a tidy hand at least." He rolled his sleeve up to show Mark a ragged scar. "This was sewn up by a drunk in the dark with his left hand." Wolf took a bite of the stale bread he picked from a basket. "Well, maybe it wasn't that dark." He grinned at Mark. "Thanks, you are a much better man than I am. I wouldn't have thought of a healer. Warriors live or die."

They ate in silence until Wolf felt he'd eaten enough.

"I need to exercise," Wolf said, "I feel slow and stupid."

"You did sleep for two days," Mark said.

"Did I now?" Wolf pushed himself away from the table and forced himself to his feet. "You'll have to take it easy on me then."

He stepped carefully into the space between the tables and Rolph's seat, took a deep breath and focused.

"Just hands, now," Wolf said and rocked forward on his toes. Mark threw a soft punch in Wolf's general direction.

"Harder," Wolf said, "throw the punch from your hip." He blocked the next couple of punches. "Faster," he said as he swayed out of the way of Mark's hand. "Your target isn't me, it's behind me." He stepped aside, "That's better, now put some moves together, throwing one punch at a time is wasteful of your energy."

They kept sparring. Mark grew in confidence as Wolf gave him advice, but never mocked him. Wolf was shifting position on the floor and blocking punches, but he worked at it now. A sweat was beading on his forehead, and the dullness of two day's sleep was being burned off. He started throwing punches back. Slow enough for Mark to handle them easily.

"Come, old man," Mark said. "If you were really that slow, the Thing would be chewing your bones."

Wolf grinned and stepped up the pace, Mark was still holding his own, but sweat appeared on the younger man's face. Wolf increased his speed again. Now Mark was in trouble, but he refused to give ground. He dodged and spun to keep away from Wolf's hands. Then Mark switched tactics and grabbed Wolf's hand and pulled him forward. He twisted under Wolf and used his arm as a lever to throw him over his hip. Wolf landed on his back, but he twisted his hand to grip Marks arm and with a foot launched Mark over his head.

At first Wolf feared that he'd hurt the young man, but then he realized that Mark was laughing, and Wolf joined in.

"If you've pulled any stitches," Cherry said from the doorway, "I'm not putting them back in."

"Your handiwork is much better quality than that, my lady," Wolf said as he came to his feet. He offered a hand to Mark. "I give you thanks for the healing." Wolf bowed to Cherry. The young woman looked like she thought she was being mocked. "You are a gift," Wolf continued, "warriors come in hundreds, but a healer is worth all of them."

Cherry didn't reply, but she nodded her head then felt Wolf's forehead and nodded again. She walked over to sit in her seat beside Rolph's chair.

"Warriors may come in hundreds," she said as she arranged her skirts, "but I doubt many are like you. My father is with his friend, but he has commanded that we have a feast to celebrate your victory over the Thing."

"Your father is gracious," Wolf said.

"It appears that the Weeds have heard that you are visiting our Hall. They have asked to send a delegation under truce to meet you."

Wolf nodded. He didn't bother asking whether the Gats were sending anyone. His Chief had made it clear that Wolf was welcome to live his life anywhere but with his own people.

"I had better find a better shirt," Wolf said as he fingered a tear in the sleeve. "I am as hard on my clothes as I am on my skin."

"I will gladly sew up your skin, warrior, but not your shirts."

"I will find you a shirt," Mark said as he looked at the tears in his own shirt.

He led Wolf to the store rooms.

"Cherry has changed," Mark said.

"Having a purpose in life will do that," Wolf said. "When she was just Rolph's spoiled daughter she had no amusement but to cause trouble. Healing Igor has given her a place apart from her father."

Mark nodded and handed Wolf a shirt. It was black with black embroidery around the hem and neck. Wolf tried it on, and it fit like it was made for him. Mark found a plainer shirt for himself.

The Hall was packed that night. The eight Weeds were seated at the table nearest Rolph. A table had been brought in and set by Rolph's seat. Wolf, Cherry, Mark and Igor joined the Chief at his meal. Wolf placed the green sword on a bench in view of everyone.

Rolph's people had outdone themselves. They had plates of meat and bread to satisfy even the lowest person in the room. Beer flowed like water. The men and one woman from the Weeds were relaxed and enjoying themselves. Warriors told of battles from various viewpoints, and there was a lot of laughter.

When the plates were mostly empty, and the beer mugs had been refilled, Rolph stood to talk. He banged his cup on the table to get the room's attention.

"As you know," he said when he had quiet, "a Thing visited our Hall and killed our men. Wolf here came to try himself against the Thing. He was the first to wound it and then led two others to find its lair. Igor lost his arm to a swamp monster, but Mark killed the monster and retrieved Igor. He regrettably lost his knife in the process." The room laughed, and Mark shrugged. "It is a choice that puts me in his debt."

"My daughter, Cherry, tended to Igor's wound, and without her expertise, I would have lost my friend and right hand man." Rolph lifted his glass in salute to Cherry and the hall cheered for her. Wolf noticed her holding Igor's hand and saw Mark noticing too. He didn't see any jealousy on the young man's face.

"Wolf and Mark returned to the Thing's lair where Wolf killed the creature and brought its head here. I would have put it on display, but you wouldn't have enjoyed your meal nearly as much. I owe a debt to both men."

Rolph pulled something out from under his seat and Wolf saw a shock of recognition go through Igor. It didn't look like much. It was a glass cube, just small enough to sit comfortably on Rolph's hand. He set it on the table; for an instant Wolf thought he saw stars shining in its depth.

"I saw the Thing leave this on the road when mad Frida disturbed him. Anyone who knows Frida, can attest to the need to give her lots of space." The hall laughed again, mostly the Duns who knew the old blind woman. "She told me when I picked it up that it would bring me fame and grief in equal measure. This cube is what helped create the hall that we live in. It is its power that lit our lights until we salvaged enough batteries to do the work. A wise man might have left the cube for the Thing to recover. Instead Wolf the warrior freed us from that unnatural creature-"

The window at the far end of the Hall exploded inward. A Thing came into the Hall and screeched. There were shouts as men scrambled out of its way and shots as some started shooting at it. Wolf thought it was the Thing back from the dead, but then he saw how it moved and knew this was a different one. This one was a wolf to the Thing's dog. It screeched again and pointed something at Rolph. Mark pushed Rolph out of the way as Igor dragged Cherry behind the table. Rolph's chair exploded in splinters as Wolf dove over the table, snatching up the cube in one hand and the green sword in the other.

The Weeds jumped up on the dais and formed a line between Rolph and the Thing.

"Get everybody out of here," Wolf said before he took a running leap to land on the table and charge toward the Thing warrior.

This thing had a belt with what had to be weapons hanging from it. Scales covered its arms and torso. It put the stick it held in its belt and drew its own weapon as it raced toward Wolf. Any person that was too close felt the edge of the sword. Wolf knew men like this, who would kill for the sheer pleasure of it. As always, he found himself in battle, not in the killing.

He shouted and gestured as if he were going to strike the cube with the sword. The Thing hissed and stopped its careless slaughter to run straight at Wolf.

Exhaustion already weighted Wolf's arms and legs. His earlier wounds pulled at him. His legs were lead, his arms wood. It didn't matter. He would live or die. The same choice that faced him in every battle. He pushed his weariness away and shouted a Gat battle cry.

A split second before they met Wolf dove along the table and rolled to swing the green sword above him. The Thing jumped over his blade and made its own attack. But Wolf had rolled to his feet and blocked with his blade. It was time to find out what this blade could take. At some level, he knew that the Hall had cleared to the edges as warriors and others watched a battle that was beyond anything they'd imagined.

The Thing and Wolf traded blows. The swords rang like glass but refused to shatter. Its arms and shoulders were similar enough to Wolf's that he knew what it could do and what it couldn't. At least he hoped so.

The Thing made a high jump and Wolf jumped to the next table. This was no closed space where the Thing could use walls to redirect its attack. They continued the fight up and down the tables; leaping from one to another. The swords clashed and banged.

Then Wolf slipped on a plate and fell to the table. The Thing was on him in a second. He parried the blow, but lost his sword and rolled off the table. The Thing jumped down and picked up the sword. It put it in a scabbard on its back, then bared its teeth at Wolf and jumped to the attack.

Wolf blocked with the only thing he had available, the glass cube in his hand. The cube exploded in a flash of light. Wolf wasn't sure he had a left hand anymore. It felt like it was simply gone. The Thing wailed and dropped its sword to pull out the rod it had tried to use on Rolph. Wolf dove under the table as a blast of hot air scorched the spot he'd been standing. He stood up under the table, and the Thing jumped off. The leap was off balance and Wolf could see that it was going to land badly. He snatched the sword from the floor and rushed the Thing. It was faster than he expected and caught its balance and pointed the stick at Wolf. He threw the sword at the Thing and rolled under the table, but not before he felt a burn down the length of his back. The Thing had jumped off the table, but Wolf had no intention of trying to put it off balance again. Instead, he kicked out at the strange weapon in the Thing's hand. His foot connected and sent the stick skittering across the floor. The Thing reached over its back to draw the sword, but Wolf used his momentum to spin around behind the Thing. He gripped the Thing's neck with both hands and with a shout he flipped it over his head to crash on a table. The Thing screeched and let go of its half-drawn sword. In one swift move, Wolf pulled the sword and beheaded the Thing. He staggered out of the way of its deadly blood, then fell to the floor. He tried to get up but the floor refused to relax its grip, and he plunged into darkness.

*****

Wolf stretched and felt the old burn scar pull. Even after a decade it reminded him of that battle with the Thing. That battle opened doors that no one in the hall that day imagined.

Mark wiggled a hand sign at him, patience. Wolf wondered when he'd lost the skill of waiting. Perhaps he was only good for waiting for battle.

Not for this. He saw the first of the Gats scouts slip out of the ruins and stand guard on either side of the road. Others joined them until they formed a corridor of warriors facing out toward danger. Every fourth was turned inward in acknowledgement that danger came from within too.

The world wasn't as dangerous as it had been ten years ago. Mark had negotiated from the brief truce that visit from the Weeds to a permanent peace. Dun and Weed together had scoured the city looking for more traces of the Things. They found none. Wolf looked at him out of the corner of his eye. It was hard to believe the young warrior was a father and a respected diplomat. Today was Mark's work.

Wolf's attention snapped back to the Gats as the guards came to attention. Gwythin walked between the honour guard on the arm of a boy at the cusp of manhood. He was the new Chief of the Gats; Liam, Gwythin's son. A younger boy walked on Gwythin's other side. Patrick was blonde as his mother, but Liam had his father's dark looks. They were both handsome and stood straight. Wolf could see, that even in ceremony, that Liam walked lightly.

"It's time," Mark said. He stepped forward with an unhurried tread. Wolf fought to keep from running to Gwythin and throwing himself at her feet. He hadn't set eyes on her in more than ten years, but his heart pounded and his palms sweated. The Weeds stood in their formation watching, and Wolf knew that Cherry and Igor watched from behind representing Rolph. Of all the people in this place, only Mark and Wolf moved. They crossed the open space and entered the corridor of honour guards. Each guard turned as Wolf and Mark passed so one in four was facing out. Ceremonial they might be, but this was their Chief they guarded.

Wolf stopped three paces from Gwythin and her two boys. He placed his weapons on the ground. Shotgun, pistol and knives. He saw Liam's mouth twitch as the pile grew larger. Finally, Wolf took the green blade from his back. He carried it in the scabbard he'd taken from the warrior Thing; his hand on the balance point of the blade. Wolf stepped forward and knelt in front of Liam and offered the boy the blade.

"There are but two of these blades in all the world," Liam said. His voice was the gentle soprano of his mother, "and you are offering it to me?"

"I am," Wolf said.

"May I draw it?" Wolf saw excitement in the boy's eyes, but also a thoughtfulness. Drawing a blade unannounced could be misunderstood. Gwythin gave the tiniest of nods. "Let us see this wonder," Liam said in a clear carrying tone. He drew the blade and examined it closely, then held it for his younger brother to see. When they had both looked at it, Liam held it high. "See Wolf's sword, Thingbane," he said and Wolf heard the echo off the walls around them. He returned it to the scabbard and then in a move that surprised Wolf, the boy handed it back to him. "Keep it for me, warrior, until it is time for me to carry it with honour."

"Thingbane!" the honour guard shouted as Wolf accepted the blade back from the boy. The lad had planned it. His grin gave him away. Liam would be a great leader. The shout was taken up by the Weeds and the Duns too until the courtyard trembled and the vibration tickled Wolf's feet. He couldn't remember any battle being as loud.

"They don't shout for a sword, no matter how pretty," Gwythin stepped forward and took Wolf's hand. "They shout for you." She urged him to his feet and lifted his hand. The shouts grew louder yet. Wolf barely heard them for the wonder of feeling Gwythin's warm hand in his.

"Liam is likely to be a brilliant chief," Wolf said to her.

"He takes after his father," she said and squeezed his hand. She turned so they were facing Liam and Patrick.

"My Chief," Gwythin said, "I beg you to allow Wolf to return to his home and his people."

"Will you put your sword arm under my command?" Liam asked Wolf.

"I will serve you with my life," Wolf said, "and when my life is done, I will serve you with my death."

Liam reached out and took Wolf's hand and gripped it tight.

"Welcome home, warrior of the Gats." There was more cheering and the honour guard switched positions again.

"Now," Liam said in a more casual voice, "I would like to meet my friends from the Weeds and the Duns. Walk with me, warrior."

The feast they held in the courtyard lasted for three days. Mark's eldest son, Wolf, attached himself to Liam and Patrick. The boys ran and played as if the three tribes had never been enemies.

"I am pleased for you," Cherry said. Her daughter stayed close by her mother, but she carried a bag that looked very much like the one where Cherry kept her medicines. "I will miss you in our Hall, as will my father."

"You are kind," Wolf said, "I will visit as my Chief allows."

"He does look like his father," she said. "I see he has some wisdom too."

When the feast was done, Mark had created another peace treaty between all three tribes. Now it was time to return home. Liam refused to let Wolf away from his side. Gwythin let her hand brush against Wolf's and he burned with his desire.

The Gats made their home not far from the swamp in the courtyard of three story buildings. The wood and brick in the outer windows were a testament to the violence of the old days, but the glass in the inner windows was whole.

"Mother will see to your lodging," Liam said when they arrived. He winked at Wolf before running off to check on his dog.

Wolf woke beside Gwythin and realized that he had never known what it was to be happy before this moment. Perhaps, he wondered, that made him the warrior he was - that he had nothing to lose. He turned on his side and filled his heart with the beauty of the woman beside him.

"So," Gwythin said, "are you just going to stare?" She smiled at him, and all the years fell away. They were kids again, pledging their undying love before the reality of the world tore them apart.

"I hope Liam doesn't expect us early for breakfast," Wolf said and reached for her.

"I was kind of hoping for a late lunch," she said before she kissed him.

Wolf fit himself into the community. The older warriors all remembered him. At Liam's insistence, he helped with the training of both Liam and Patrick. Only the old Chief's jealousy had kept Wolf away. Now that he was home, his face carried a smile more often than not. Wolf took to training the boys not just in weapons, but in how not to use them.

"Talking first," he said, "brings no dishonour on a warrior, and if talking fails, you can always fight later."

Mark came for a visit with Athena, the woman warrior who had come to that banquet ten years before and fallen for Mark before she returned home. Little Wolf ran off to find Liam and Patrick.

"Little scamp," Mark said, "he's been pestering me for a visit for months."

"I'll have to thank him then," Wolf said. "He's a fine boy and likely to grow to be a fine man like his father."

"So, are you finally happy, my old friend?"

"Delirious," Wolf said.

"Remember the witch?" Mark said, "She got it right all the way along; except for you."

"What do you mean?" Wolf said.

"She said when you found your heart's desire, your life would end."

"No," Wolf said, "she said I would find my heart's desire after I died."

"Right," Mark said, "what could you want more than what you have?" Wolf wasn't paying attention. He was watching the boys running and playing. Little Wolf had fallen and was trying not to cry. Liam had his arm around the smaller boy's shoulder and was whispering something that made Little Wolf laugh. Then they were off again.

That night while he lay in Gwythin's arms Wolf saw an odd light outside the window. He disentangled himself and went to look. A strange beast floated through the air. Lights searched the ground and the roof. There was a flash and Wolf saw a man on the roof fall.

"Gwythin," Wolf said, "we're under attack. The Things are back in force. Get everyone out. Use the tunnels. Don't look back. Warn the Weeds and the Duns."

"Here's your sword," she said as she held it to him.

"Give it to Liam," Wolf said, "tell him it's time."

She pushed the tears away from her face and ran out of the room. He heard her calling the alarm. Even in peace the people knew what to do. They only needed minutes to empty all the buildings and get to safety. Wolf peered through the window again. The beast floated over the building to his right and he saw Things dropping from a hole in its belly. It was up to Wolf to buy his people those minutes.

He reached beneath his gear and found the Thing's other weapon. After the fight in the Hall, no one had thought to look for it. Days afterward, Mark had given it to Wolf and made him promise to keep it secret. Holding the rod, Wolf ran toward the stairs and battle.

At the stairs, he found Liam with the warriors. They were encouraging the last few people down the stairs.

"This building is empty," Liam said. "It is time to take the battle to the enemy."

"With any other enemy," Wolf said, "you'd be right, but these Things are not hurt by our weapons."

"I have Thingbane," Liam said.

"Yes," Wolf said, "and you must use it to defend your people. You are their Chief, lead them bravely, son."

Liam looked at Wolf for a long moment and Wolf thought he was going to argue, but then the young man saluted him with the sword.

"Yes, Father, die well," he said in the traditional last order of a Chief to his warriors before battle. He vanished down the stairs with half of the warriors.

"These Things are fast and strong," Wolf said to the others, "but their bones are weak. Use edged weapons or these." He lifted the rod he was holding. "Our firearms do nothing against them." They nodded, and he led them up the stairs to battle.

The Things on the roof were the warrior Things.

"As I shoot them," Wolf said, "take their weapons and use them." He showed them the tiny depression on the rod that fired the deadly beam.

He killed three Things before they knew he was there, but there were a dozen more on the roof and they were shooting back now. The Gats warriors were familiar with the roof and were holding their own, but more Things poured from the belly of the beast. Wolf left the Gats to the fight and started making his way along the roof. He held the rod in his left hand and a sword in his right.

Wolf had wondered if being happy would make him a worse warrior, but he was deadlier than he'd ever been. Joy strengthened his arm and carried him through the battle. Even with the new Things joining each second, the warriors were holding their own.

Ropes hung from the beast and Things swarmed down them. Wolf dashed up to the nearest rope and started to climb it. His warriors concentrated their fire on the other ropes and up into the ship. They paid a terrible price as the Things on the roof flanked the warriors. The battle had turned; the Things were winning.

Wolf was in a hall. Things ran at him, and he shot them down. His rod failed; he picked up another, and then another. The walls around him burned while a screeching siren blistered his ears. Wolf ran along the hall shooting anything that moved in the smoke.

He reached a pair of doors that were locked. The rods did nothing to them, but the green sword shattered them open. He had already jumped to the side as beams shot out at him, then Things charged through. He cut them down with his sword then rolled into the room. There were Things running about, but none had weapons.

The room was dark and lit from screens that flashed red. The Things were pushing buttons and obviously trying to get the fire in the belly of the beast under control. Above them was a cube of the same glass as the one that Rolph had given him. Wolf wondered if it would explode the same way as the smaller one had. There was only one way to find out. He ran to climb onto the platform and looked up at the cube.

He saw the sword appear out of his chest before he felt it. Wolf turned and cut down the Thing that had stabbed him. Then his heart stopped. *It would have been nice to have a son.* Wolf's world started fading. Then he remembered Cherry's comment that Liam looked like his father, and Liam calling him father and saluting him.

Wolf smiled and with every bit of his remaining strength swung the sword up to strike the cube.

*****

Liam walked rear guard behind his people. His mother carried Patrick. Mark walked beside him. They reached the large cave before the tunnel's end. Liam set guards at the tunnel and went to the opening. He looked out into the night of a world. It was dangerous in new ways. Then the night turned to day. Stark shadows ran away from them deep into the city. They slowly faded, and the light became the red light of fire.

"We'll stay here until daylight," Liam said. "Then I'll lead a team to see what happened."

***

Liam, Mark and six other warriors stood on the edge of a crater where their homes once stood. There was no sign of the Beast or the Things.

"Thingbane!" Liam shouted as he saluted with the green sword.

"Thingbane!" shouted the other warriors.

"Come," Liam said, "let's go make a world to make Wolf proud."

Sparkles and Blood

Other Books

Alex McGilvery

Fake Blood

Blood covered everything.

The blond chick in the white T-shirt screamed and danced around like she'd seen a mouse. She was supposed to be screaming because her boyfriend had just been decapitated. Martin hoped that the director wasn't really paying attention.

"Cut!' Quentin banged his hand on the arm of his director's chair. He immediately tried to hide the fact that he'd hurt himself. "This is a horror film, you stupid cow!" he said as he walked through the blood bath. "You need to look horrified. Not like some girl who got a bug down her cleavage." He demonstrated the little dance that Clarisse had been doing. It was funny really, as long as you weren't Clarisse. It was too bad that his five-hundred-dollar wingtip shoes didn't have better tread.

He slipped in the fake blood, and his feet took out Clarisse. She landed on top of him and was swearing like a trucker as she peeled herself off the director. Martin would have expected some noise from him as well, but he was silent. The special effects man didn't think anything short of death would stop that mouth.

Turns out he was right. Quentin had cracked his skull wide open on the terrazzo floor of the school they were using for a set. Martin smelled the change in the air before he noticed the slightly darker colour leaking from behind the director's head. All the fake gore looked ridiculous next to a little of the real thing.

Clarisse started screaming again. This time Quentin would have been delighted. She was a regular Faye Ray once she got going. Martin swore under his breath and walked back to his truck.

He climbed up into the camper that sat on his truck, closed the door, then sat cross legged on the bunk and started his yoga routine. The shaking in his gut gradually slowed and dissipated. He was as addicted to yoga as he had ever been to the booze. The upside to the yoga was that it didn't show up on a breathalyzer. He hated death, which made his chosen career of faking death a little odd.

He was half way through the routine when the assistant director banged on the door.

"Martin," Brad shouted and banged some more, "cops are here. They want to talk to you."

All the calm of the yoga left Martin in an instant. He stood up and climbed out of the camper. Brad was hopping from one foot to the other.

"You have to explain that it was an accident. Clarisse didn't mean it."

"Right," Martin said, "why me?"

"You're the special effects guy. It's your blood all over the place. Well not your blood but…"

"Easy, Brad," Martin patted him on the shoulder, "I know what you mean." He left Brad dithering behind him and went to face the music.

The police were taking pictures and samples of all the blood and everything else. Martin recognized the officer in charge.

"Fancy seeing you here," the officer said.

"I'm sure my parole officer informed you that I was gainfully employed."

"Don't you find fake murder tame after the real thing?"

"It's a job." Martin said and tried to relax his hands. "I'm good at it." Detective Philson could always get his blood pressure up.

"I'm sure you are," Philson ran his finger through the fake gore. "But you should know that blood isn't really this colour."

"If you make it darker, it looks fake on screen."

"Really?" Philson said and looked for something to wipe his hand on. Martin tossed him a rag from his pocket. "So you spread this all over the place and hope no one falls and kills themselves?"

"Clarisse was on her mark," Martin pointed to a space on the floor that was clear of blood. "So she wouldn't slip. All she had to do was scream." He crouched down by where Quentin lay and waved at the shoes. "The director walked through the scene with leather soled shoes and tried to do a sissy dance. He slipped and fell. Clarisse fell on top of him. End of director, end of movie."

"What happened to 'The show must go on'?" Philson said.

"It isn't my show," Martin said.

"So it was just an accident?"

"Just a stupid accident."

"Like that other stupid accident."

"That wasn't an accident," Martin said, "it was murder. You proved that, remember?"

Philson waved his hand and Martin took it as a dismissal. He didn't think that Philson was going to try to make anything out of this. The man just liked to pull Martin's chain at every opportunity.

After the police left, the health and safety people came and looked at the set up. Martin showed how he'd created a safe mark for Clarisse with clear silicone on the floor. They tried to find something to complain about, but the set was made for the actors on their marks, not for a director in overpriced shoes. What finally sent them away was the video on youtube of the entire rant and its lethal conclusion.

A suit showed up shortly after that and expressed the producer's regret, but the project was being scrapped. Twenty minutes after that Martin's truck was packed and he hit the road. He had no illusions about any money from that fiasco ever showing up in his bank account.

Bloodless

Martin stretched, then stared at the roof of his camper just above his head. In a couple of minutes, he would paw through the last of the change in the ashtray and see if there was enough to buy a coffee at McDonalds. For now, he wanted to get the self-pity out of the way.

In the month since Quentin died in a puddle of Martin's fake blood, not one director would even talk to him. Nobody wanted him. It didn't help that the rumour mill said Martin had posted that video of Quentin. The show rags had done a touching tribute to the director which failed to mention any of his faults. They had also done a piece on Martin which outlined the whole case that had put him away for ten years of hard time. They failed to mention that he'd been out and clean for three years.

That was enough for today. Martin sat up and crossed his legs. His head was a fraction of an inch from the ceiling. These campers weren't made with six foot ex-cons in mind. He centered himself and let his breathing wash all the resentment from him. If he was going to get a job today, he'd have to have a smile on his face.

"Martinez," Paul shouted at him, "pick it up and get those skids unloaded." Martin breathed through his clenched teeth and started moving boxes off the skids. Paul had hired him for under

219

minimum wage and charged him for every day that Martin parked his truck behind the store. The night manager was under the assumption that Martin was illegal. Martin didn't argue. He was paid in cash and an illegal immigrant was a step up from ex-con.

He vaguely remembered his grandfather's stories of coming to the U.S., but neither Martin nor his mother spoke any Spanish. Martin picked up a few words from the real illegals that came and went. He figured most of them were cuss words. The morning took its time coming, but Martin finished his shift and wandered up to the McDonalds.

"Buenos dias," Gabriela said as she poured him his coffee. She winked at him. It had taken her only one look at Martin to see he was no illegal, but she'd kept his secret. She had her green card and worked at two different jobs to pay the bills for her and her son while her husband went to school to get his electrician's papers.

"Morning," Martin said, "how did Sam's test go?"

"He passed!" Gabriela smiled broadly. "As soon as he gets his papers, he can look for work."

"Terrific," Martin wrote on the back of his receipt. "This is my mother's phone number. She'll know where people are hiring. She's Alicia Roderick."

"If your mother can help Sam, why can't she help you?"

"I'm a sad disappointment to my mother. She refuses to help me." Martin blew on his coffee and took a sip. "As a penance she helps whoever I send her way."

"Gabriela!" her manager shouted from the back, "there are paying customers waiting!" Martin winked at her and took his coffee away. Gabriela smiled brightly at the empty store.

"Next!" she said. She waved the scrap of paper and put it in her pocket.

Martin took his coffee out to his truck to drink it. He almost spilled it when his cell phone rang.

"Hello," he said, "Martin here."

"Thank God, you finally answered," a familiar voice said.

"Brad?" Martin looked at the missed calls; twenty-seven missed calls. This might mean money. "I'm a little busy right now, keep it short."

"I need you," Brad said. "My special effects guy just quit on us. I need a replacement by noon or we'll go behind schedule and the producer will have me skinned and staked out on an ant hill."

"That sounds painful," Martin said.

"He showed me the ant hill," Brad said. "It's huge!"

"How do I find you?" Martin grabbed a paper and pencil. "I'll be there in an hour," he said after he copied Brad's directions. He was pretty sure he knew the place. The truck started with a satisfying rumble and he headed out of town. As he drove Martin tried to calculate how to translate Brad's desperation into a bigger fee.

Bloody Hard

The set was on the back end of someone's ranch. A clapboard cottage sat at the far end of a meadow filled with wildflowers. At the near end a trailer park clashed with the rustic scene. Brad was sitting on the step of the trailer marked 'assistant director's assistant'. He brightened up as soon as he saw Martin. Before he could get out of the truck, Brad ran over and climbed into the passenger seat.

"Pull in over there," Brad pointed to the end of the ragged line of trailers. The pecking order on the set was clear from the size of the trailers. It was also clear that Martin would be the bottom of the heap. He didn't care, as long as he got paid.

"So, what's the deal?" Martin said.

"First," Brad said, "I have to tell you that the director absolutely refused to even think about hiring you."

"So, what am I doing here?" Martin went to put his truck into reverse, but Brad put his hand on Martin's. Martin just stared at him until the hand was removed.

"Please," Brad said, "I doubt that he even knows what you look like. I told him your name was Rodrigo Martinez, and you were a special effects guy from south of the border."

Martin tried to speak, but it came out as a growl.

"I'll pay you ten percent above what Quentin paid, twenty!"

"Ok," Martin said, "I'll put on my best Mexican accent. What's the work?"

"We're making a vampire movie…"

"So, blood then."

"Not really," Brad said, "these aren't that kind of vampire. These ones sparkle."

"Since when do vampires sparkle?"

"Never mind, just think of it as chick horror, heavy on the chick, light on the horror."

"So, no blood."

"Maybe a little, but not much." Brad shrugged. "What we need is for the vampires to spark when they fight. Like a flint on an empty lighter."

"Let me think about it," Martin said, "why doesn't he just do it in post? Not that I mind the work."

"The director's a purist. Doesn't like computer effects."

"Joy," Martin said. "As long as his money's good. Now go away and let me think."

"Don't think too long," Brad said, "we're shooting in two hours." He jumped out of the truck and ran away.

Martin got out of his truck and climbed into the camper. He opened his effects cupboard and stared at what he had. He might just be able to pull this off.

***

"So, you put the patch on wherever you want the sparks and put the makeup over it to hide it. It fires just like a squib."

"What about fire?"

"If you aren't covered in gasoline, you should be just fine." Martin showed the actors his hand and fired the patch. It was just a downsized version of a ricochet squib. The actors' eyes went wide, and he had to put one on each of them to prove that it didn't hurt.

"How many have you got?" The dark-haired actor said.

"Enough for a few takes," Martin said. "Screw up too much, and we all get staked to that ant hill."

"Good enough for me," the blond one said.

"Buenos dias, Rodrigo," a cultured voice said from behind Martin. It took a moment to remember that he was Rodrigo. He turned around to see a man who was a bit taller than he was. If it was possible to have custom made jeans and western shirts, Martin was sure he was looking at them.

"Buenos dias, señor," he said. The man in the jeans winced.

"Let's just forget the Spanish shall we?" he said. "I'll just pretend that someone didn't hire the notorious director killer behind my back. Call me Bill."

"Works for me, Bill," Martin said. He explained the flashers to the director and the actors were sent off to get set for the first take.

They shot the fight behind the cabin under the trees. Martin let the fight coordinator fire the sparks. They got the scene in two takes.

"Impressive," Bill said as he watched the actors head for the canteen. "You show up without a clue what we're doing and produce exactly what I need. How many of those things do you have?"

"I can make more and reuse the patches."

"Brad," Bill said, "go ask those gentlemen to preserve the patches when they take off the make-up."

"Yes, sir." Brad trotted off.

"He's a good assistant," Bill said, "gives me what I need even if I don't want it." He slapped Martin on the shoulder. "Remind me to buy you a drink of your choice."

"I don't drink," Martin said.

"Ah, how many years?"

"Three."

"I'm still working on my first," Bill said. "Bloody hard with all these drinkers about."

"Sometimes it is just bloody hard," Martin said.

Brad came back with his hand full of patches which Martin took from him. He picked up the remote from the fight coordinator and headed back to his cabin to reload them.

There was a knock on the door. It didn't sound like Brad so Martin stretched the kinks out of his back and pushed it open. Bill was standing with two plates in his hands. Martin could see thick steaks steaming in what was now evening air.

"I come bearing gifts," Bill said, "you saved me a pot load of money. I gave Brad a bonus, but I thought you might enjoy a steak dinner."

"Come on in," Martin said. He cleared a space on the table and set out mismatched cutlery and poured water.

"My father had a camper like this." Bill waved his fork.

"This was my father's camper," Martin said.

"Maybe we're brothers," Bill hoisted his cup and they dug into the meal.

"Ah, I needed that," Bill pushed away the scraped clean plate.

"I've been eating McDonalds for the past month," Martin said. "My stomach thinks it's died and gone to heaven."

Bill laughed. "I'm extra glad I thought of this then, but I have to admit I have an ulterior motive."

"Yes?" Martin said. He wanted to be wary, but he felt just too damned good.

"My sponsor is back in Hollywood and the cell signal out here is crappy at best," Bill stopped and looked at the table. "If I need someone to talk to…"

"I'll be here," Martin said. "Like you said, we could be brothers."

"Thanks, Martin," Bill stacked the dishes carefully.

Martin watched the other man carry the dishes back toward the Director's trailer. That's the first director I've met who was human. He folded the bed out and sat cross legged. As he began his yoga he put all concerns aside to center himself. Brad had a long list of miracles for him to pull off tomorrow. He'd need all the focus he could get.

In the Blood

"Look," Martin said, "I can make a nice boom and blow up all kinds of dirt from that hole, but no one is going to be in it when I do."

Myrna smiled brightly at him.

"I'm sure you can do it safely," she said as if she hadn't heard a thing he said.

"No one is in the hole when the charges go off," Martin said.

Myrna stopped smiling. She pulled out the radio that she had at her belt.

"Hi, Bill," she said, "I've got a teensy problem with the shoot here. The pyro guy won't let me do the shoot my way." Her jaw clenched as she listened to Bill on the other end. "I want him to blow the hole, then Winter climbs out of the dust cloud." There was more squawking from the radio. She was glaring at Martin now. "He wants to talk to you."

"Martin."

"Don't under any circumstances allow that girl to talk you into anything dangerous. You figure it out. I don't want to come out and shoot that scene myself."

"What did he say?" Myrna said.

"We do it my way," Martin tossed her the radio. "We're shooting from this angle, right?" He walked over to where the camera was set up. "Then the secondaries will get him climbing out of the hole."

"Fine," Myrna threw the radio at him. "You direct the shot." She stomped off into the woods.

Martin picked up the radio and clipped it to his belt.

"You heard the lady," he said. "Let's get this done." He walked around to the far side of the hole. It wasn't that deep. It wasn't going to take a big charge to make dirt and dust fly. "So the idea is that you fall down from there and hit the ground, creating this hole."

"That's the idea. We've already done the green screen for the fall," Winter said. "We just need to shoot the poof and me climbing out."

"So we don't have to have you in the hole, just climbing out." Martin pulled a charge out of his toolbox. "Let me give this a try. Cameras on the hole. I'll count the blast then roll into the hole from the back side here. I want to see how it looks."

He put the charge in the hole then lay about four feet from the edge.

"Earplugs people!" He checked his. "Cameras on, blast in three, two, one." The bang was muffled through the plugs. He rolled into the hole and in a few seconds got to his feet and stepped out. Dirt was still falling around him as he saw the camera through the dust.

"Looks pretty damned good," the camera operator said as she played it back for Martin.

"Well if you can do it," Winter said, "I guess I can."

"It will be exactly the same charge," Martin said. "You don't have to rush; you'll have time to make it look good. The rest is editing."

"You wouldn't make a bad director," Winter said.

"Tell me that after we get the shot," Martin slapped the actor on the shoulder.

The second blast worked just as well as the first, and Martin had to admit that Winter made climbing out of that hole look very good.

"Ok, folks," Martin said after he'd reviewed the tape on all three cameras. "We do a couple more for luck then pack it up and go get lunch."

"Where did you learn to direct?" the camera operator said.

"From bad directors," Martin said, "I would always think about how I would do the shot."

"Nice," she said. "Name's Olivia."

"Martin."

"Hey," one of the other operators said, "there's bits of bone in the hole!"

"Probably animal bones," Winter said. "They've got to die somewhere."

The camera operator shrugged his shoulders and turned to pack up his camera.

Bill came over to the trailer that evening with salmon steaks.

"You want a promotion?" He said as he sat down. "That was some very good work."

"I'll stick to what I know," Martin said, "I don't need the stress." Bill laughed and they ate their dinners.

"So if you don't mind my asking, why do you have your dad's camper?"

"He's dead," Martin said, "he didn't need it anymore."

"Right," Bill said, "changing the subject now. How did you learn all this special effects stuff?"

"There was a guy in prison. He got me started on it. He showed me how to mix fake blood and do gushing wounds. All that stuff. He told me about the different kinds of bangers, but the guards were reluctant to give me gunpowder to practice with. I spent a lot of time in an old quarry learning how to rig bangers and not blow myself up. I picked up the rest here and there watching others work."

"Well, however you learned, you are a fine effects man."

"Thanks," Martin said. "How did you get into directing?"

"I was a really lousy actor, but the business is in my blood," Bill said, "so directing was the only way for me to stay in film. So far it's worked out for me."

After Bill had left with the plates, Martin sat on his bed before he started his yoga. Maybe he

should give directing a shot. Then he shook his
head and started his breathing.

First Blood

Martin was half way asleep when there was a frenzied banging on the door of his camper. He sat up and peered through the tiny window. Myrna was standing outside with a bottle in one hand. She took a swig as she hammered on his door with her other. He pulled on his pants and a shirt. He had no interest in facing a drunk woman in his boxers. He took a deep breath then pushed the door open.

The door pushed Myrna back, and she sat hard on the ground. She upended the bottle over her mouth then threw it at Martin. She had surprisingly good aim for being so drunk, but Martin got his arm up in time to protect his face. The bottle bounced off him and smashed against the door of his trailer.

"You could give a girl some warning," Myrna said as she tried to stand. Martin sighed and grabbed his shoes. He put them on before picking his way over to give her a hand up. As soon as she was on her feet she threw herself at Martin and tried to kiss him. The alcohol on her breath sent danger signals through him. He pushed her away a little harder than he intended.

"Wha', " she said, "don't you want any of this?" She pulled her blouse open to reveal ample breasts. "Don't get much of this in the big house, do you?" She tried to get close to Martin again, but he put up his hand.

"Please just go to bed," he said.

"You some kind of effing gay?" Myrna laughed and wiggled in what she must have thought was an erotic manner. "You must have been real popular." She wrapped herself up again without buttoning the shirt. "Just my luck," she muttered, "two effing directors and they're both effing gay." She wandered away in what Martin hoped was the direction of her trailer.

He closed the door to his camper and tossed his shoes in the corner before heading back to bed. His right foot landed on a shard of glass from the bottle. He stumbled into the wall and banged his head. He felt like the miasma of Myrna's breath still hung around him. He realized that the bottle hadn't been completely empty.

Martin sat on the bed and pulled needle-nose pliers from his work drawer. He used them to extract the glass. It hadn't gone in too deeply, so he taped it up and put on a clean sock. When he was done with that he fetched his broom and meticulously swept every corner of his camper free of glass. He'd have to do something with the glass outside in the morning.

He awoke with a start sometime later. He didn't know what woke him, but his heart was pounding, and he was gasping for air. Martin sat on the bed and went through every yoga routine he knew before he started to relax. By then the sky in the east was beginning to lighten.

He was picking up the remains of the bottle when Bill came by.

"Have you seen Myrna?" Bill said.

"Not since she banged on my door drunk and angry," Martin said. "She left just as drunk and even angrier. She complained about being on a set with two directors and both of them gay."

"Ah, yes," Bill looked down, "she tried to seduce me and was very insulting when I refused her. But I am gay. It is what drove a wedge between my father and me."

"I was wondering more about the two directors part, than the gay part."

"Oh, right," Bill looked up at Martin. "I warned her that if she tried anymore shots that put the actors, or anyone else, in danger I would fire her and make you director."

Martin shook his head.

"I told you that I didn't want to direct."

"Martin," Bill said, "everyone wants to direct. I'll get one of the women to check Myrna's trailer. If she was that drunk she'll be useless all morning, so you're on. Meet me in fifteen at the canteen and we'll go over the shooting list for today.

Martin put the glass in the garbage and headed over to the canteen. He didn't want to direct, but he felt an undercurrent of excitement that made him wonder if he was lying to himself.

The actors and crew were standing around the canteen with coffee or an alternative. Martin grabbed a tea and poured lots of sugar and milk in. There was a single lonely muffin on a tray so he slathered butter on it and tried to pretend that it wasn't like eating paper.

"Ok, gang," Bill said as he joined them, "Myrna is not around this morning. She's not in her trailer, so unless one of you wants to go to your trailer to wake her up..." He paused as some of the actors shrugged, but no one moved. "Fine, so Martin will be doing the filler shots today. Brad, you have the shot list so you'll assist. Take crew two for cameras. The rest of us have some dialogue to shoot." He clapped his hands. "Let's go people."

"You're directing?" Brad said. Martin could see the younger man's jaw clenching and unclenching.

"It's not my idea," he said, "I'm really going to need your help today. Let's show Bill what we can do."

"We?"

"Absolutely," Martin said, "and I will make sure that Bill knows just how vital you are to the work." He saw Brad relax and flip to the first page of the shot list.

"What we want," he said as he read through the list, "is a lot of shots of different areas and scenes that the editors can use for transition shots. We need to stay well away from where Bill is shooting. We can use ambient sound as well."

"What do you think we should do first?"

Brad looked around and pointed over to the forest on the west edge of the meadow.

"Would I sound too artsy if I said that the light over there should be perfect?"

"I'd say you'd sound like a director."

They walked around the edge of the meadow with the sound and camera crew following them.

"Bill doesn't want people walking through the meadow until we need to," Brad said.

Martin saw what Brad meant about the light as beams from the morning sun slanted through the trees. They set up cameras and took film from a variety of angles. Martin had them do a close-up of some tiny white flowers. They got lots of audio of birds and the sounds of a tiny brook. Bill and his team were shooting on the far side of the cottage and were out of sight so they got some long shots of the cottage in morning light.

It was exacting work. Martin had to make sure that the angle was usable and that none of the crew showed up, or anything else for that matter. He had to reshoot one set because he saw a shadow in the corner of the frame on playback.

Bill wanted some dark woods mood shots. So once they were done in that part of the woods they walked back around the meadow, then deeper into the woods.

"The forest is thicker here," Martin said, "there will be some good tangles and such in here."

"How do you know?" Brad said as he picked his way over the uneven ground.

"I spent a lot of time in the woods as a kid," Martin said.

The camera crew was having a harder time of it. One of them slipped on a mossy root and went to his knees.

"Careful!" Brad said, but the camera man wasn't paying attention. He was scrambling back and falling over. The camera fell on the moss as the man lunged for a log and vomited on the other side of it. Martin walked over to see what had upset the man. Myrna lay on the other side of a log. Her neck was obviously broken as her head lay at an impossible angle. Her throat gaped open and blood covered the breasts that she had waved at him last night. The blood wasn't from her throat though. It was from the gaping wound where her heart used to be.

"Brad," Martin said, "take the crew back, then go call the police."

He listened to them as they crashed their way back to the trailers. It never failed to amaze him how noisy people were in the woods. He looked back at the body of the woman. He tried to decide how he felt, but the only thing he knew for sure was that if he'd been setting the scene; he'd have used a lot more blood.

Bloodsuckers

The police arrived in the form of Detective Philson.

"You really have a thing for dead people," Philson said as he arrived at where Martin leaned against a tree.

"Dead people are your job," Martin said, "I just make them look dead."

"Right," the detective said, "except for when they get dead for real."

Martin didn't bother answering as the Detective peered at the corpse. The other officers were setting up cameras and opening sample cases so Martin decided it was time for him to leave.

"Don't go far," Philson said without looking up, "I'll have questions for you."

"Of course," Martin said and walked back to his camper. When he got there, he realized he didn't want to be alone so he walked to the canteen. The whole crew was there along with Bill's crew. Brad wasn't saying anything, but the rest were engaged in wild speculation; partly about what caused her death, but mostly about whose trailer she'd slept in last night.

Martin sat down and refused to get drawn into the conversation. He was on his second cup of tea when Philson found him.

"M.E. says it was probably a mountain lion." He helped himself to a cup of coffee. He tasted it and put another spoonful of sugar in. "It'd be the first mountain lion I ever heard of that tore its victim's blouse off before eating."

"She tore her own blouse," Martin said. "She banged on my trailer and offered a view of her breasts. She was extremely drunk."

"Right, and finding her womanly wiles wasted on you, she wandered off to get eaten by a mountain lion. They'll attack anything warm blooded."

"I'll walk you to your car, detective." Martin put his tea down. They walked in silence to Philson's car.

"Strange mountain lion to eat the heart and nothing else," Martin said as Philson climbed into his car.

"Not nothing else," Philson said. "The M.E. said there wasn't nearly enough blood, so either she was killed somewhere else and dumped there, or that was one thirsty mountain lion." He looked out the car window at Martin. "Don't go anywhere." He rolled the window up and drove away.

Martin walked back to the canteen. The actors and crew looked at Martin. He picked up his tea, but it was cold. He put it back down.

"Philson and I have some history," he said. "You should be happy. If he's going to pin anything on anyone, it will be me."

The next few days were busy enough to push Martin's unease to the back of his mind. He was working with Brad on the second crew doing small scenes that Bill didn't think needed his personal touch. A lot of them involved special effects, especially the flashers he'd made for the fight scenes.

"There are a lot of fights for a chick flick," Martin said to Brad at the end of one day as Brad handed him a bunch of patches to reload.

"They're all fighting over the girl," Brad said, "that's supposed to make it ok."

"Right," Martin said, "so I reload these and we should be able to shoot the night scene?"

"Yes," Brad said and looked at his clipboard. "It's where we did the blast in the hole. The fight coordinator has been spending all day re-blocking the fight. Someone dug a bunch of holes in the ground around the blast hole. We've had some people fill them in and rake them, but he's worried about the soft ground."

"Ok," Martin looked at the sheets in his hand. "Two cameras are on tripods and two free hand." He tried to imagine the setting. "I'm going to have to look at the setting again for the cameras. I'll get these done and back to makeup. The fight guy will control the flashers. We just have to make sure that the cameras work."

"If it were only that easy." Brad said.

Martin loaded flashers the rest of the afternoon. The sky was just turning dark when he handed them over to makeup. This scene was the most complicated that Bill expected Martin to direct. Martin kept trying to push the directing onto Brad, but Bill was adamant.

So while he continued to think that Brad deserved the assistant director slot, Martin was technically calling the shots.

He headed over to where the crew was setting up cameras and lights. He checked the locations against the paper in his hand and moved one of the cameras because a tree was leaning into the shot. Maybe the holes in the ground had something to do with the tree.

"Ok folks," Martin said when the crew was set. "We are going to shoot this a lot of times with different lighting. I want to see the flashes, but I also want to see who is winning the fight. We wouldn't want the wrong people to win and have to reshoot the movie."

The actors arrived from makeup and stood waiting for his direction.

"Look," Martin said, "you know the routine. It's a fight and there is a risk. Stick to your blocking and you'll be fine. The fight coordinator, ah, Chuck here, is going to run you through the fight a couple of times. Take it slow until you're ready. Then we'll do a run at full speed before we start shooting with the flashers. We start at full lights and gradually dial down. We've got grey filters on the cameras so we don't need to go full dark. I don't want you getting hurt. Questions?"

"Yeah, whose idea was this?"

"I know it wasn't in the original script, but you guys looked so good with the flashers that the producers had this fight scene written in. They're signing the checks, so here we are." Martin waited a beat, then said, "Ok, let's get this done, I'm missing my beauty sleep."

The dry runs went perfectly. Brad looked worried, he'd told Martin that a perfect rehearsal meant a disastrous shoot. Martin swatted a mosquito.

"Let's try it for real," he said. "Places, Chuck you have the controller? This is for real. Lights on full, camera, action."

At first it looked good, the actors were warmed up and on their marks. But Chuck was off on timing the flashes.

"I can't see with these lights," he said, "I've got spots everywhere."

"Someone get him a hat or something," Martin said, "let's reset and do it again."

"It's a good thing I loaded every flasher we have," Martin said after they were on their fourth take. He decided that they would take the lights down a notch. Maybe that would help Chuck with the timing. At first it looked like it was working, then Winter put his foot in a hole and fell.

"Cut!" Martin went over to check him out.

"I'm good," Winter said, "just a little cut on my hand from a sharp rock."

He got it bandaged and they tried again, and again.

"Ok, I'm down to my last batch of flashers," Martin said. "If we don't get it right this time we come back out tomorrow and do it over." There were groans all around and people swatting bugs.

"Damned bloodsuckers," someone muttered.

"Silence now," Martin said. "Lights at twenty-five, camera, action!"

Maybe it was the threat of redoing the scene the next night but the fight went perfectly. Martin yelled "Cut!" and everybody cheered, until a scream came from one of the camera operators.

"Full lights!" Martin shouted and looked to where the camera operator was supposed to be standing. The camera lay on the ground with the red record light on, but no operator.

"Damn it, Neil," yelled Olivia, "enough of your jokes!" She walked over to the camera and picked it up. "If this thing's damaged; it's coming out of your paycheck."

That was when something black hit the woman and she fell back into the light. She dropped the camera again and held her throat where blood leaked between her fingers. There were shouts from the rest of the crew and some looked like they were going to run. Chuck ran and tried to stem the flow of blood.

"Stay here," Martin said, "whatever it is can see in the dark a lot better than you can."

Everybody crowded together in the light.

"Who has the keys to the quad?" Martin said. He wanted to fall apart with everyone else, but he was director, they were his responsibility.

"That would be Neil," someone said, "fat lot of good that does us."

"Anyone know how to hot wire one of those things?"

"Those lights won't last long," one of the crew said, "they'll burn out."

"We turn half of them off and let them cool; then we switch," Martin said. He pulled out the radio. It looked a lot darker with only half the light but the movie people huddled in the small pool of safety and waited for rescue. He noticed that the lead operator's hands had fallen from her throat and the blood had stopped flowing. Chuck swore softly. Martin didn't say anything. He swatted a mosquito.

"We have a problem," Martin said.

"It had better be a damned good one!"

"I'm guessing that one dead and one missing counts as a damn good problem," Martin said. He reminded himself to breathe. It wouldn't do anyone any good if he and Bill got into a fight. They needed to get everyone back safely.

"Damn," Bill said. "What happened?" Martin gave him a quick update.

"I'll come and get you," Bill said.

He showed up a few minutes later with the other quad and equipment trailer.

"Everybody get on the trailer or the back of the quad. Leave the equipment, we'll get it in the morning."

"What about Olivia?"

"She won't fit on the trailer with the crew," Bill said. "We'll cover her with a tarp and get her in the morning."

The crew didn't waste any time piling onto the trailer and the quad.

"I'll walk," Martin said. "Just go slow enough for me to keep up."

Bill just nodded and turned the quad in a circle around Olivia's tarp covered body. Martin half walked, half jogged beside the quad. He couldn't hear anything above the noise of the engine.

Martin wasn't sure if that was a good thing or not.

Blue Blood

Detective Philson wasn't happy. He hadn't been happy since his second wife had run off with her shooting instructor. He figured the amount he paid in alimony was worth the peace and quiet. That was five years ago - the peace and quiet had become boredom.

Like many men in his position he married his job. His job paid overtime, neither of his wives did. That was why he was the one sitting in the police station doing paperwork when the call came in from the movie shoot. He looked at his watch. It was three in the morning.

"What kind of trouble are you getting into now, Martin?" he said after he told dispatch that he would take the call. As he climbed into his car, he thought about the first time he saw Martin. He'd been a skinny little punk. The kid had been covered in blood. He had this strange expression on his face like he was either trying not to cry, or trying hard to.

The story was simple. He and his dad were camping like they did a lot of. In that same crappy rig that Martin still used. The dad had left Martin to watch the fire while he watered some trees. Martin's story was that his dad had jumped out at him to scare him. It was unfortunate that Martin had been splitting wood and instinctively split his dad open. Both Martin and his dad were more than a little intoxicated.

That was fine until Philson got the M.E.'s report. Mr. Roderick had been hit no less than ten times and the fatal blow was to the back of the head. It went from a stupid accident to murder. Philson had found some stuff about the late Mr. Roderick that gave him a great deal of sympathy for Martin, but murder was murder.

Philson had put a word in the D.A.'s ear, and the sentence was oddly light. Martin had got out after ten years and Philson made it his hobby to keep an eye on the man. He'd never tell Martin, but he was secretly proud that he'd made good in the last three years.

That's what made this business at the movie shoot so disturbing. If it came out that anything criminal was going on, Martin would be the one everyone pointed their fingers at.

He pulled into the field of trailers and it looked like a circus all lit up for a show. Every light in the place was on. He found them all huddled in the canteen tent.

"Ok," he said, "where's the body?"

"We thought it best to leave her until morning," the head guy said, Bill was his name. Philson couldn't remember his last name.

"That so?" Philson said. "I think I'd like to go and see the scene now."

"That's not a good idea," one of the crew members said. He took a slug from a bottle he was holding like a teddy bear. "There's something out there killing people."

"I have a gun," Philson reminded him as he patted his holster.

"You'll want the shotgun along just in case," Martin said.

"In case of what?" Philson said.

"Just bring the damned shotgun," Martin said.

"Ok, ok," Philson lifted his hands. He and Martin and Bill went back to his car and fetched the shotgun and a big flashlight. They unhooked the trailer and Philson rode behind Bill while Martin sat on the rack and faced the back. As they rounded the cabin the lights in the woods went on.

"They won't last that long," Bill said, "so whatever you need to do, do quickly."

Philson saw the tarp and knew something was wrong. It was way too flat to have a body beneath it.

Bill must have seen it too, because he started swearing under his breath. They pulled up beside the tarp and Martin jumped off. Philson handed him the shotgun and turned the flashlight on. Martin cycled a shell into the chamber and followed behind and to the left of Philson like he'd gone to cop school. Bill stayed on the quad and kept the motor running.

"There are no drag marks," Philson said as he peered at the ground around the tarp. "Either something carried her away or she walked away. Are you sure she was dead?"

"Her throat was torn out," Martin said, "same as Myrna's. She'd stopped bleeding and had no pulse."

"So something carried her away, leaving no prints and no drag marks," Philson said, "just peachy." He walked deeper into the woods. He heard Martin start to say something then stop. The flashlight lit the forest as bright as day, but only in a narrow beam. Still he saw something that looked like a body.

"Over there," he said and shone the light on the body. He walked over to the spot and realized that it was a man. His throat had been ripped out, and his clothes shredded over his chest. Like the other woman, his heart looked to have been ripped from his body.

"Neil," Martin said, "a practical joker. No one ever laughed at his jokes."

"Poor guy," Philson said. "If this is Neil, where is Olivia?" He shone his flashlight through the trees, but he didn't see any other bodies. There was the snap of a twig breaking. He spun and aimed his light in that direction.

His fingers tried to pull the trigger of his gun even though he was still holding the light. He couldn't let go of the flashlight, just kept uselessly pulling a trigger that wasn't there.

"Olivia!" Martin said. "What happened to you?"

Philson tried to tell him to shoot the creature. He could see the bones in her neck through the hole. There was no way that she should be alive. Finally, he gave up on his right hand and fumbled the gun out with his left. They trained for this kind of thing, but in the training his hands weren't shaking and he didn't have his heart trying to implode. The first shot hit the ground between him and the creature. She was trying to make some kind of noise, but she couldn't with no throat. The second shot hit her leg, but it might as well have missed for the good it did.

"Philson," Martin shouted, "what are you doing?"

The third shot hit her hip and still didn't slow her. Philson tried to step back, but tripped over something and fell to the ground. He finally let go of the flash light and got his right hand on the gun. He emptied the gun into the creature as it jumped on top of him and bit his throat. He kept pulling the trigger and hearing the click of the firing pin. He tried to yell something to Martin, but nothing came out but a gurgle.

The last thing he heard was the blast of the shotgun again and again, but each one sounded further away until the only thing he heard was the sound of his heart stopping.

Blood Burns

Martin stood with the smoking shotgun in his hands and stared in horror at the hole right through Olivia. He could see Philson's vest through it. If he'd been faster…but he'd thought that somehow the camera operator was alive. He didn't know why Philson was shooting at her until it was too late. It was like that other night; he was too slow to understand.

"Run, Billy!" he said.

"I'm not running anywhere," Bill said. Martin shook himself and looked at Bill.

"Sorry, I was in a different place."

"You can visit your happy place later," Bill said, "we have to get them to help."

"There's no help for Olivia," Martin said and rolled her body off Philson, "But we may be able to help Philson." He picked up the police officer with a grunt and carried him back toward the quad. Bill picked up the flash and followed. By the time he caught up Martin had sat on the rack and was holding on to Philson.

"Drive," he said.

Bill careened through the woods to the canteen. All the crew were still there. They helped lift Philson to a table.

"He isn't breathing," Bill said, "and there's no pulse. We'll work on him. Someone drive to the hill and call for help."

Martin threw open the first aid kit and found the resuscitation kit. Tearing the plastic off he put the mask on Philson and started breaths while Bill did compressions. He noticed when someone else took over compressions so he handed over the breathing to Chuck. He was so light headed that he missed the chair and sat on the ground. He decided to stay there. Damn, he should have stayed at Walmart. It sucked, but nobody died.

It wasn't until he felt a hand on his shoulder that he realized that he was sobbing uncontrollably. Martin didn't care. He sat there and let whoever keep their hand there.

"He's back!" someone shouted and Martin surged to his feet. Brad jumped back, but Martin didn't take the time to say thanks. He ran to Philson.

"He's not breathing," Chuck said, but he stepped aside to let Martin lean over the man.

"He's got a pulse, I think," Winter said and staggered over to sit down.

Philson pulled the mask from his mouth.

"Burns," he said, barely loud enough for Martin to hear him.

"I'm here," Martin said.

"I know," Philson said. Martin thought he was talking about the present, so he grabbed Philson's hand and squeezed. "I talked to Billy, too late. Proud of you." Martin felt the tears coming again and focused on his breathing. He wasn't

255

going to break down in front of this man. He heard sirens coming in the distance.

"I know," Martin said, "I know."

"Thirsty," Philson said.

"Here's some water," Chuck said, "not too much."

"Not water," Philson knocked the water away. "Blood!" He bared his teeth and lunged at Chuck. The fight coordinator spun out of the way, and Philson staggered against the stove. Martin watched him stare at the flames that licked their way up Philson's sleeve. Then the cop snatched a bottle from a crew member and poured it over himself. The flames erupted to cover his whole body and he staggered away from the canteen.

Martin watched as the first man who ever believed in him walked, burning like a straw effigy toward the flashing red and blue lights of the people who were coming too late to save him.

***

The sun was up, and they were out of fire extinguishers. The police and the paramedics had emptied them one by one over Philson, but as soon as they stopped he burst into flames again. Martin and the rest stood a horrific final watch until the last flame blew out, and only ashes lay on the road.

By this time more police had arrived including a black truck with a full SWAT team. A team went to retrieve Neil and Olivia. They came back with Neil and reported that all they found of

Olivia was ashes. Martin knew they'd been in the right area because they had the shotgun and the .38.

"I want some answers." The cop had lots of chevrons and gold braids on his uniform. Martin guessed he was the Chief or something.

"I wish I had them," Martin said, "I really do, but I already told you what happened." He was too numb to care what he said to the cops.

"People coming back from the dead and spontaneously combusting. That's not an explanation, that's a fairy tale!"

"Captain," one of the SWAT team said, "we have the camera from the scene, maybe there's something on them."

"You're welcome to use our equipment to view the film," Bill said.

It only took a minute to hook the camera up. They checked the end of the shot, but all that was on them was the fight scene. Martin could tell that Bill wanted a better look at it, but the police made them switch to the next and the next. The last camera's battery was dead, so one of the techs swapped another battery in. As they looked at the picture, Martin could see that it was the tarp, lying empty on the ground. The tech moved the picture back in time, and it was just the empty tarp, until something shambled in reverse out of the woods and crawled under the tarp.

They watched it in forward and reverse a half dozen times. It was clearly Olivia, moving under her own power. It was also clear that her throat was ripped wide open.

"No one could live with that kind of injury," the Captain said. "Are you movie people messing with us?"

"None of us here have the knowledge or ability to do that," Bill said. "It would take the CG people weeks to come up with that, and it wouldn't look that real."

"Wind it further back," Martin said, "she was holding the camera when the thing attacked her. Maybe the camera picked it up." The Captain glared at Martin but nodded to the tech.

They watched time reverse from where she crawled out from under the tarp. Now they watched an unmoving body under the tarp. Then they saw the quad reverse into the clearing, the crew jump off and the tarp pulled from the body. Suddenly she was alive and holding her throat while the crew peered into the woods behind the camera. She was standing, then walking backwards toward the camera. The frame tilted and spun as she picked it up from where it had been dropped. In that second Martin saw something move, then the moment passed as the camera was on the ground again.

"Let it go forward, slowly," Martin said.

"Shut it, boy," the Captain said, "I'm in charge now." The tech had already started the camera in forward at half speed and the Captain didn't make him stop. They watched as the camera was picked up, then that flash. The tech froze before Martin could say anything.

"Holy sh.." someone said. Martin understood. He wanted to swear too. The shape was blurry as if it had been moving too fast for the camera to focus. All they could see was that it was on two legs, and barely distinguishable where the head was, a line of what Martin was sure were snarling fangs.

Blood Bath

Martin and Bill spent the morning arguing with the police. They wanted to stay and see this thing through. The police wanted everybody gone.

"There is close to a hundred thousand dollars' worth of equipment here," Bill said. "I plan on staying and keeping an eye on it."

"Look at all the cops," the Captain said. "Do you really think that someone is going to walk up and steal it while we are here?"

"Let me call my producers," Bill said. That was easier said than done since the only cell signal was on a hill a mile and a half away. Finally, they patched him through one of the patrol cars.

"Hello," Bill said, "I need to speak to Mr. Lohengrin ... Yes, it's Bill. Things have gotten very complicated. The police want us to vacate the premises... No, we don't have time to pack the equipment...The crew is gone already…Yes, I see…Right, thank you, sir."

Bill climbed out of the car. "Mr Lohengrin stated very emphatically that we are to cooperate in every way possible with the police. We are to vacate the site as soon as you sign for all the equipment. Any damages incurred will be the responsibility of your department."

Martin thought the Captain was going explode on the spot. He radioed the Chief and had a long conversation in the car. They couldn't hear what he was saying, but it involved a lot of hand waving.

"The Chief says you can stay, but you sign a release, and if you get hurt, you're on your own. If you get in the way, I'll arrest you and figure out charges later."

Bill and Martin quickly signed the hastily scribbled release forms and went to the canteen. The squad leader for the SWAT team rolled his eyes at them, but didn't interrupt his briefing of his team and the other officers who were standing with them. He waved his hand. They headed off in all directions.

"I suppose you think you're going to be heroes?" the team leader said.

"No," Martin said, "we're here to safeguard the equipment and make coffee."

"Well then," the team leader said, "get to it. Call me Sargent Truscot."

Martin preferred tea over coffee. His father had liked coffee and was very particular about how Martin made it. He drank coffee because it made a link between him and Sargent Truscot, however tenuous. He put extra sugar in it and thought of Philson. He raised his coffee cup and mentally toasted the cop.

Truscot went to the SWAT truck where the equipment was to track his teams. The search went on all day. Nobody saw anything, though one trigger happy rookie blew a squirrel to kingdom come. The Captain came and drank coffee, but said nothing. As soon as the cup was empty he went back to his car. Truscot called in the teams before sunset.

"Ok," he said, "I know you've been walking around all afternoon. So here's what we're going to do. These fine gentlemen will rustle up some supper for you, then you're going to walk around all night. There's a cop killer out there, and we're going find him, fill him full of holes, then arrest him so they can hang the S.O.B."

Martin had already started on supper. Bill was designated chopper for the salad. There was a huge grill so Martin just threw meat onto it until it was covered. He had everything almost cooked when the last team returned.

"Hey, rookie, maybe he'll cook your squirrel for you!"

"Only if you skin it first," Martin said. "Who likes their steaks rare, and who wants them all buggered up?"

Martin did dishes while Sargent Truscot briefed the teams again.

"You've got a sense of the lay of the land," he said. "Remember that. Whatever this thing is, it moves fast. So keep your eyes peeled. SWAT, use your infrared. Don't use flashlights, you won't be able to see anything. There's near enough a full moon, use it. Don't get trigger happy. I don't want anybody to get shot by our own guys. If you see this killer, take it down. Use your training and we'll all see morning."

The teams went out quietly and quickly. Once again Sargent Truscot could follow their progress by the cameras on the SWAT helmets. This time he invited Martin and Bill to join him in the truck.

"Don't say anything, don't touch anything. If anyone asks, you were never here."

They found seats where they were out of the way and still could see a little of the screens.

"Zone One, clear."

"Zone Three, clear."

"Zone Two, the rookie fell into the bog."

The teams checked in and moved to the next space on the grid. Nothing happened more exciting than the rookie's stumble until just after eleven.

"Team Six here, I think I saw something!"

"Affirmative," Truscot said. "Be careful."

"Holy crap!" someone said.

"No chatter!" Truscot said. Then they heard gunfire and shouting.

"I shot it, but it's still coming!" There was more gunfire, then a scream that was cut short.

"Team Five, Six is in trouble. Get over there. Extreme caution."

"Tell them to aim for the heart," Martin said.

"What?" Truscot looked up at Martin.

"Olivia didn't stop until I shot her heart."

"All teams, all teams, target the heart. Repeat, target the heart."

"Team Five in position. There's no sign of Team Six, damn!' More shots and shouts.

"Team Three here, we see something. In pursuit."

"Team One here, will back up"

"Head bearing 276 degrees, Team One," Truscot said. "Be sure of your target. Team Four, report, report Team Four.

"Team Four, Bryson's down, I'm in the bog up to my neck, but I don't think it sees me. Oh sh.., sorry Sarg, but it just ripped Bryson open and ate his heart." They heard rapid shooting. "God, it won't die."

"The heart, damn it, shoot the heart!"

"It's down," Martin heard, then the sound of the rookie being sick.

"Teams, check in," Truscot said. "Check in." There was nothing but gasping and the occasional shot. Curses and more shooting, then screams and nothing.

Bloody Hell

"Team Four, here" came the rookie's voice, "I'm going to stay right where I am until the sun comes up."

"I hear you, Team Four," Truscot said. "Stay alert." He sagged and put his head on his desk. He pushed himself upright after a moment and turned to the monitors.

"You movie people are used to reviewing video," he said. "Come here and watch. Let's see if we can learn anything from this effing mess."

"Go back to where Team Six saw something," Martin said. "Can you play it back slowly? Those things are fast."

"Here are the controls," Truscot said and showed them. "You can make them do anything you want."

"Almost as good as our setup," Bill said as he sat himself by the desk. "It would make more sense for each of us to take two teams, we can switch if we don't see anything."

"Good," Truscot said and pushed a few buttons. "You're at that desk, and Martin over here."

Martin sat down and familiarized himself with the control system, then reversed back before the first sighting. He followed the jumpy video forward as the team walked through the woods, scanning for trouble. They were steady and disciplined. There was a flash of movement up ahead and suddenly the camera was leaping and weaving forward. The quiet conversation became frantic and disorganized. There was another flash of movement ahead, then something struck from the side. The camera spun wildly but for a brief second it showed the face of the attacker. Martin froze it on that frame.

He reminded himself to breathe. He took air in and let it out until he thought he could speak without his voice breaking.

"I've got something," he said. The others paused their videos and came to look. The face wasn't sharp, but it was clear enough. It was a man's face, but a man who had been stripped of all softness. The bones were all but bursting through the skin. The eyes were just black pits. What was most disturbing was the open snarl that revealed teeth that were sharp and deadly.

"It's an effing vampire," Truscot said. "How the HELL am I supposed to explain to the Captain that we had our collective asses handed to us by an effing vampire?"

"More than one," Martin said. "There was a decoy up ahead, then this one attacked." He sat back in the chair. "How are your men trained to follow a dangerous suspect?"

"They're supposed to keep the suspect in sight," Truscot said, "but wait for back up to engage. Fire from a distance if need be."

"I think whatever was out there," Martin said, "was affecting your men's minds. As soon as they saw the movement it was like they lost all discipline. That made it much easier to ambush them."

"Bloody hell," Truscot said. "Those were our best people, and they acted like rookies. I've got to report to the Captain." He pushed himself to his feet like he'd aged twenty years. "Stay in here. It's safer."

"You can't go out there alone," Bill said, "it isn't safe."

"It isn't the vampires I'm worried about," Truscot said, "the Captain is probably going to shoot me where I stand. He's not tolerant of failure."

"All the more reason for us to come," Martin said. "We can relate how you died bravely."

Truscot rolled his eyes, but he didn't protest when Martin and Bill followed him. Martin took a wooden pole from below a tarp.

"You called them vampires," he said, "maybe a wooden stake is a good idea." Truscot shook his head, but Bill fetched the other pole. They'd been sharpened to fit through the grommet in the plastic tarp.

"Just keep them out of sight of the Captain," Truscot said. "I don't want him shooting you, too."

They walked along the gravel past the parked cars of the officers who lay dead in the woods. The

Captain's car was bigger, but lacked the roof top lights. There was a dim light in the car. When they got closer Martin could see that the side window was shattered. Truscot drew his weapon and his flashlight. The light showed the blood spattered over the Captains face and the interior of his car. The faint glow came from the part of the screen of the laptop that wasn't drenched in the Captain's blood. There was a gaping hole in his chest.

"Damn," Truscot said, "so much for the guys who said the Captain never had a heart."

"Hearts," Martin said. "They take the hearts from their victims. Except Olivia, because we were there. They didn't like the lights. She came back. How hard would it be for these creatures to get at the hearts of your officers through their vests?"

"Damn near impossible," Truscot said. "But I would have said vampires were impossible too."

Martin saw a flash of movement ahead, between two cars. Truscot saw it too because he snapped his gun forward and started running toward the movement. Martin felt his pulse race and he wanted to sprint after Truscot and get there first. Bill was already charging and holding his pole like a spear. Martin forced his feelings away and dashed after them. He tried to remember how long between the sighting and the attack on the video. Ten seconds? Five? He ran and felt a push to run harder, the enemy was ahead.

Martin spun and lowered his spear as a shadow lunged out at him. The point found the gap between the vampire's teeth and lodged in the back of its throat. The urge was gone and the thing screamed past the stick. It slashed at the pole and snapped it off. Martin lunged again and pushed the vampire back against a car. The clawed fingers slashed at the stick again and turned it to splinters. It tore the wood from its mouth and lunged again at Martin. He fell back and a long pole came over his shoulder and buried itself in the thing's heart. It screamed even louder and tried to pull the spear out, but Truscot added his weight to Bill's. They pushed the vampire to the ground, and then pushed the wood through into the gravel.

Martin heard an answering growl from not too far away.

"Time to go," he shouted, "there's another one." He picked up the three-foot section of the pole that the creature had pulled from its throat.

They ran back toward the trailer. This time Martin's feet felt heavy, like he couldn't move. He saw the other two struggling. He was going to die. Martin turned and screamed defiance. The vampire stopped just ten feet away. Martin held the pole like a knife and lunged toward the creature. It took a step back, then Truscot opened fire from the side. Chunks of flesh flew off the creature and it ran off between the cars.

"Into the trailer," Martin said.

They climbed in and barred the door from the inside.

"Good God," Bill said, "they're moving. The cameras are moving again."

Truscot stared at the screens which showed lumbering progress through the woods.

"Report!" he said into the mike. "All teams, report." There was no response. No sound except the rustle of leaves and the crack of branches snapping.

"Sargent" came the whispered voice of the rookie, "B-b-bryson just g-g-got up and left. It l-l-looks like he's heading b-back to you."

"Ten-four," Truscot said, "stay where you are."

"Negative, Sargent," came the whisper, "If I d-d-don't move, I'm g-going to freeze to death anyway."

"Stay low," Truscot said. "Only a heart shot will stop one of them. Your bullets aren't going to get through the vests."

The rookie didn't reply. The cameras showed the teams making slow progress toward the camp. Martin didn't know what to expect when they arrived. He hoped that door was secure. He stopped himself from going and checking.

The first camera showed the trailers, then the second one did too. There was no sign of the blindingly fast attacks of the other vampires.

Martin thought of Philson. These would still kill just as dead.

Truscot turned on an outside camera in time for them to see two of the shambling officers attack each other. Others joined in until it was hard to know how many were involved in the fight. Somehow their memory and knowledge was lost. They did terrible damage to each other and from the howls and screams they felt the pain, but none showed any of the training that a police officer would have. Though Martin was sure they all had knives, no weapons but fists and teeth were used.

One dropped, then another, they were still moving but too badly damaged to stay on their feet. Martin wondered if the fight were going to last forever, when he noticed the scene was getting lighter. The first rays from the sun hit the fighters and their screams took on a new note. Their skin reddened instantly, blistered then sloughed off in sheets. They turned and made for the trees, but fell to the ground. The flames started at their hands and faces, but soon consumed everything but their weapons and badges.

Truscot put his head on the desk and wept. Martin didn't blame him.

There was movement from the edge of the forest and he steeled himself for more horror, but the figure limped into the sun and didn't burn. Martin opened the door and went to help the rookie to safety.

Bloody Fools

Martin watched Constable Reba Pierce sitting across from him and sipping coffee. Martin thought Bill was making something for breakfast. Truscot sat at the end of the table and watched the rookie with worried eyes. No one said anything, they didn't talk about the sunny weather, or the birds singing from the edge of the woods. They especially didn't talk about the piles of ash that was all that remained of heavily armed and well trained police squad that had arrived the day before.

Bill placed plates in front of the two officers, then fetched plates for himself and Martin.

"Eat," he said, "you're going to need it."

Truscot ate mechanically as if it didn't matter what he put in his mouth. Reba pushed the food around on her plate. Martin ate slowly and savoured the flavours. It was just bacon and eggs, but it was a meal that he hadn't expected to survive to eat.

"Don't just play with the stuff," Truscot said to her, "eat, you'll need your strength to make some kind of report of this effing disaster."

"I don't think we should bring more people in just yet," Martin said.

"I'd nuke the place if I could," Truscot said.

"But we can't," Martin said, "and bringing more people in will just expose more people to the

situation. We can't fight them on their own terms.
We have to fight our way."

"And what way is that?" Truscot said, "hiding
out in a trailer?" He went back to demolishing his
breakfast. Reba had started hers, and apparently
decided she was hungry after all, her plate was
almost empty.

"What do we know about these vampires?
They are killed by a shot, or a stake through the
heart." He counted on his fingers. "They are fast
and work together, but they don't come up with
new strategies quickly. All the ambushes were
essentially the same, almost down to the second.
They have some way of affecting our minds,
clouding our judgement. They burn in the sun." He
thought of the pile of ash between the two cars with
a blackened pole still stuck into it.

"If they burn in the sun," Reba said as she
looked up from mopping the last crumb from
his plate, "they need a place to hide during the
day."

"So we find the place they hide in and tear
their effing hearts out," Truscot said. "But we were
all over this place and there are no caves.

"The holes," Martin said. "They were buried
in the holes, behind the cabin. The blasts from the
filming must have woke them up."

"So we go through the woods with a shovel
and dig them up?" Truscot snorted. "Who knows
where they are."

"I thought I saw something going back toward the cabin," Reba said. "I can't be sure."

"You have shovels?" Truscot looked at Bill.

"How do you think we dig holes?" Bill said.

Truscot armed himself and Reba with shotguns from the trailer. Martin and Bill carried shovels. They took the quads back to where the holes were. Bill didn't think that they looked any different than they had before, but they picked a hole and started digging.

"There are eleven holes plus the big one," Bill said. "We killed one, so that means ten left."

"Wonderful," Truscot said, "we not only have vampires, we have an infestation of them."

They dug in silence after that. Trading off between shoveling and standing guard. Even though they knew the vampires couldn't go into the sun, they still felt like they were being watched.

The first hole they went down to where the soil suddenly got hard. It was almost four feet deep. There was no body in it. There was nothing in the next one or the one after that.

"I have the feeling that they aren't in here," Reba said, "but I'm sure I saw them come this way."

"How much do you know about the cabin?" Martin asked.

"We haven't used it much," Bill said. "The interiors were shot in the studio. The place is pretty much abandoned. It isn't nearly as good on the

inside as the outside. We've been in it to shoot
Gwen leaning in the window or going in and out
the door."

They climbed back on the quads and went
back to the trailer.

"If we are going exploring out of the sun,"
Truscot said, "I want a lot more fire power. Do you
know how to shoot a shotgun?" He handed one to
Martin and Bill along with a belt full of shells.
"Never mind. You point this end at the bad guy and
pull the trigger. Keep it tucked tight against your
body, it kicks." He tossed Reba a belt. "These ones
can take six shells." He showed them how to load
them before slinging a shotgun on his back along
with a belt and a vest that had grenades hanging
from it. "Flash grenades," he said, "these things
don't like light." He had knives for them too. "If
you get close enough for knife work, you're
probably dead, but better to have them than to need
them." They each snapped a flashlight to the barrel
of their shotgun, and they were ready.

"Great," Bill said, "now all we need is some
theme music."

"If we survive," Truscot flashed a brief grin.
"I'll play it for you. It was a terrible program, but
the music was good."

As they walked back to the quads, Martin
made a detour and picked up an axe.

"Philson might have told you that I'm good with an axe," he said. The others looked at him, but Truscot shrugged.

"It's just after noon," the Sargent said, slipping into his briefing mode, "but there is no guarantee that these vampires are sleeping. So stick to the walls like glue. If they attack, make sure you keep the fire lines clear, and don't shoot each other. Martin, if you swing that axe, remember there may be people behind you. We aim for the heart. A blast from your shotgun will shred a normal human's heart. We'll just hope it does for these monsters too. You do realize that we're bloody fools and we're all going to get killed?"

With those encouraging words, they split into two groups, Truscot and Martin at the front, Reba and Bill at the rear. Truscot counted the entry, then they burst into the cabin with their shotguns pointed to the ceiling.

It was empty. Sunlight leaked through the roof and streaked the floor in the shadows. Sunlight poured in from the open windows.

"The trap door for the root cellar will probably be in a corner," Martin said. Truscot began sweeping the floor with his foot. Martin picked a different corner and did the same. Reba found the trap door.

"It looks like it's been opened recently," Reba said, "but not frequently, or all the dirt would have gone through the cracks."

Truscot used a knife to pry the trap door up while Reba kept a shotgun pointed over his shoulder at where the hole would be.

"Three, two, one," Truscot said and flipped the door all the way open. Martin caught it before it crashed on the floor. They turned on the flash lights and peered down into the cellar.

"No stairs," Truscot said, "this keeps getting better." He swung himself down into the hole in the floor and moved to the side, the beam of his flashlight covering the room.

"Clear," he called softly. "Come on down and join the party."

Martin lowered himself into the cool dank room.

"Reba, you and Bill stay sharp up there. If we need to leave in a hurry, we'll need your help."

"Right, Sarge," she said.

Martin kicked at the floor but it didn't look like it had been disturbed.

"That shelf isn't up against the wall," Truscot said. He peered behind it. "There's an opening here." He and Martin lifted the shelf to the side. "They weren't using this as their main entrance." Truscot aimed his shotgun down the hole. "They must have another entrance."

"It's daytime," Martin said, "they've got nowhere to retreat to."

"That could be dangerous," Truscot said. "Nothing is worse than a man with his back to the wall."

"I'm dangerous too," Martin said. He cycled a shell into his shotgun. "Philson made sure I never forgot it."

Truscot nodded, then led the way into the tunnel.

Alex McGilvery

Tainted Blood

The tunnel wasn't quite tall enough for them to walk upright. Martin's legs soon burned from crouching, but he couldn't hold the shotgun properly bent over. He'd left the axe in the cellar. There would be no room to use it here. The air was close and humid, and sweat kept running into his eyes. He blinked it away. He wasn't taking his hands off the shotgun.

Breathe in, breathe out, he told himself. Stay centered; alert but calm. Watch for any foreign feelings.

The tunnel smelled strange but also familiar. It smelled like the dried sausage that Billy's dad had made. They hung in the cellar. The meat was so dry that it couldn't go bad. Martin used to love that sausage. Then Martin's dad had bought a lot of the sausage, more than they could eat in a lifetime. And he'd invited Billy to go camping with them. He'd told Martin he was old enough to sleep in the cab of the truck. Martin knew what that meant. Billy didn't. So when Martin's dad had gone off to pee, Martin explained it to the boy. Then when Dad came back, he had the ax ready. He sent Billy running away while he made sure his dad would never take any more boys camping.

What tortured Martin through the trial and the years in prison was that he couldn't say for sure if he was protecting Billy or jealous of him. He saw Billy in the tunnel and he knew.

Martin's shotgun went off a fraction of a second after Truscot's. The twin blasts slowed the vampire's attack, but it kept coming. Its screeching rasped on Martin's nerves and made his hands shake. His next shot hit dead centre and cut off the noise, but now they heard more screeches and cries in what sounded like guttural language.

"Back," Truscot said as he pushed a shell into his gun. "We won't have time to reload in here."

Martin tried to walk backwards, but it was even harder than walking forward in the cramped tunnel. He loaded two shells into his shotgun. More vampires came crawling along the tunnel like giant spiders. He fired into them, but barely slowed the charge. He heard Truscot beside him firing as well. The other man was shouting something, but Martin couldn't hear it over the ringing in his ears.

Truscot pulled a grenade off his belt as Martin's gun clicked on an empty chamber. He covered his eyes at the last second and still the white light leaked around his arm and left spots of blindness. The vampires were clawing at their eyes and making noise that slashed through the ringing in Martin's head.

He reloaded his shotgun as he scrambled backwards. He fell out into the cellar and rolled to one side. Truscot came out shooting with the vampires almost on top of him. Martin snatched his axe and buried it in the chest of the nearest vampire, then kicked it away. Another took its place, and he shot it one handed. The shotgun twisted out of his hand, so he left it and swung the axe again. Reba and Bill were shooting down through the hole in the ceiling. Reba paused to take Truscot's hand and haul him up and out. Martin spun the axe in a vicious figure eight in front of him. The vampires paused for a brief second. Martin kicked the shelf over on them.

"Throw down another flash!" he yelled.

Truscot tossed the grenade down. Martin kicked it into the tangle of shelving and vampire. He waited a fraction too long to close his eyes and he was immediately blind. He reached up and miraculously found a strong hand to pull him from the cellar. He rolled away from the hole as the other three emptied their shotguns into the cellar.

When they stopped, the silence was painful.

"I make three bodies there," Truscot said through the ringing, "and there was at least one in the tunnel. That still leaves way too effing many. Let's get out in the sun."

They staggered out of the cabin and Martin was shocked that the sun had barely moved. The ringing in his ears faded enough that he could hear the others speaking. He still saw more spots than clear vision, but it too was gradually improving.

The first thing he saw was that there was something wrong with Truscot. He was holding his hand and blood poured from between his fingers.

"The effing vampire got me," he looked up at the sun. "How long do I have before I start bursting into flames?"

"I don't know," Martin said, "Philson said he burned, and then he thirsted for blood. He was still in control enough to choose to burn rather than become a vampire."

"I knew he was tough," Truscot said. "We don't have much time then; my hand is already burning. If I'm going to die, I'm going to take as many of them with me as I can."

They jumped on the quads and returned to the trailer. Truscot opened a locked cupboard and pulled out blocks of explosive. He filled the pockets of a vest with the blocks and taped more around him. He wired them all together and attached the wires to a control. "I have a switch," he said, "but it's also on a timer. It's going to blow in fifteen minutes whether I hit the switch or not. But I'm burning up, I don't think I'll make it back through the sun." Truscot sat down.

"Wait here," Martin left the trailer and fetched his truck. He backed it up to the trailer with the door of the camper open.

"Get in," he shouted, "there's no windows to let in the light." Martin felt the subtle change in weight and heard the shout. He drove forward enough for the door of the camper to close. When he heard it slam he sped toward the cabin. He backed the truck and camper right into the cabin, then heard the camper door crash open. He tried to drive away, but the trailer was jammed in the cabin. The doors had no space to open. Martin banged on the window, but all his tools were in the camper. Martin kicked at the window until it finally popped out. He dove out over the hood of his truck and ran away from the cabin.

The ground moved under his feet before he heard the explosion. He fell to the ground and held on as it shifted and bucked under him. As it stopped moving pieces of the cabin and his truck started raining down around him. Martin pushed himself upright and sprinted away. The bigger chunks fell behind him, but he was running in a downpour of dust and splinters.

When debris stopped falling on him, Martin turned and looked at the results of the explosion. There was a crater where his truck and the cabin used to be. A line of sunken ground marked the tunnel as it ran out into the meadow

"Holy crap," Bill said as he pulled up on the quad. "I thought you were a goner."

"I needed a better exit strategy," Martin said. He brushed dust from his face.

"They've all got to be dead," Bill said, "there's no way anything survived that blast."

"I want to be sure," Martin said and climbed onto the quad. "Run over to the line there and let's follow it to the end." The line of sunken earth ran arrow straight to a deep hole in the middle of the field.

"How deep is that thing?" Bill said.

"Deep enough that something might have been sheltered down there. Let's get back to the trailer. We've got work to do before sunset."

Bloody Battle

Martin looked at the armoury in the SWAT trailer. He'd like the shotgun, but having to reload every six shots could be deadly. There were lots of flash grenades, but they were a last resort. They'd buy him time, but not kill any vampires.

"How good a shot are you with that thing?" Martin said, pointing to a big rifle that was mounted on a bipod.

"I can hit a quarter at four hundred yards," Reba said. "The fifty caliber will do the job, but it's hard to hit a moving target."

"As long as you don't hit me, we're good." He pointed to another weapon that looked like an old-fashioned tommy gun.

"That's a new one," Reba said and hefted it. "It's a shotgun with a fifty-shot magazine." She picked up another magazine. "You can just change the mag, like so." She showed him how it worked.

"Why wouldn't Truscot have used this?" he said, taking it from her.

"It has a bad habit of jamming," she said, "and it kicks worse than the regular shotgun." She showed him a switch on the action. "This moves it from semi to full auto. The full auto will only go a second or two before it jams and is useless." She picked up a couple of guns that looked like oversized pistols. "These are full auto machine pistols. The rounds are light, and you go through a

285

clip in less than three seconds, but for those three seconds you will make a mess of whatever you're pointing at."

He packed up the weapons and ammo in a large black bag he found, and they carried it out to the quad. They rode out to join Bill who was scouting out the hole with the biggest pair of binoculars that Martin had ever seen.

"These are insane," he said, "I can see everything like it's full daylight down there. There are a few places that look like they might be tunnels, but no movement."

"Point out the tunnels to me," Martin said as he took the binoculars. Two were on the wall of the hole and would only be accessible by climbing up or down to them. The bottom one ran from the floor. "So if you lower me by the winch over there," he pointed to the tunnel closest to the surface, "I can check that one out. We'll have to haul me up and reset the winch for the other one. Reba can cover me with the fifty caliber. Bill, you toss flash grenades if you need to, but warn me."

Reba handed him a helmet.

"The night vision is passable on these and there is a shield to drop, for when you use the flash grenades." She showed him how it worked. "The radio will work when you're in line of sight, but once you're in the tunnels it'll be worthless."

"Let's get started," Martin said. "We're burning daylight."

He strapped on guns until he felt like he was in a cheezy war movie, then clipped the winch cable to his harness and started down the side of the hole. The first tunnel was perhaps twenty-five feet down. He reached it quickly and used a knife to anchor the cable to the side of the tunnel.

He flipped the night glasses down over his face and headed into the tunnel. The small flashlight strapped to what he thought of as the tommy shotgun lit up the dark. The tunnel was simply carved out of the dirt. There were a few places where it was shored up with beams. It went on for fifty yard before it ended in a collapse. It didn't look recent, and nothing had been digging at it. Martin retraced his steps and was hauled back up to the surface. They moved the quad and winched him down to the next tunnel.

The second tunnel was also shored up with wood, but it didn't go any further than the first did. Martin clipped himself to the cable.

"Lower me to the bottom" he said double checking his gear on the way down. There was a dark shadow on the floor. He was sure that it would be safe for the vampires to attack him. Martin wanted to be ready. The cable stopped short of the floor leaving him an eight foot drop.

"We'll bring you back up and figure something out," Reba said. That was the moment the vampire attacked from a tunnel they hadn't been able to see. It leaped up and grabbed Martin's feet and started to climb up his legs. Martin pointed the first gun he could grab at the vampire and pulled the trigger. The vampire's head vanished into dust, but the hands were still clutching Martin's feet.

"Martin," Reba yelled, "the quad is slipping, roll away to your right as soon as you hit the floor." He felt the cable slacken and bent his knees. He saw a second vampire run toward him as he hit the floor and rolled desperately away. He hit a wall and pointed his pistol at the vampire, but before he could pull the trigger the quad landed between them. It crushed the headless vampire, but sent up a huge cloud of dust that hid the other one from view. Martin unclipped himself and emptied the machine pistol into the cloud before he dropped it and grabbed a shotgun.

The vampire came through the dust with one arm hanging at its side. Martin fired his shotgun twice. Remembering his earlier experience, he was holding it tight. The blasts took off the other arm and shattered the vampire's knee. Martin took an extra split second to aim while the creature tried to balance on its one good leg. The next shot was through the heart. He could see the tunnel through the vampire before it collapsed to the ground. Martin picked up the machine pistol and changed magazines. He strapped it on again before reloading the shotgun. The longer he could use his trustworthy weapons, the better.

"I'll watch the tunnel at your back," Reba said, "Bill's gone to get the other quad and some rope. There's no winch on that one. We'll try to have your spare weapons ready for when you come out."

"Thanks," Martin said, "I'm heading in."

This tunnel was very different than the first two. It twisted and turned between two rock walls. The floor was narrow, but Martin thought he could see footprints in the loose dirt. The rock was slimy, but the moisture didn't make it to the floor, so Martin was breathing dust. It reeked like rotten meat. He flipped the night vision visor down and turned the flashlight on.

He felt like he was trapped in one of the low-resolution shooter games he played as a kid. At each turn he expected an attack, but there was nothing. He wondered how far this tunnel went into the hill. He was debating turning back and checking the other tunnel when it opened into a cave. He could just see the rock wall on the other side. He stepped into the cave and checked his right and left. It looked clear. There wasn't anywhere for anything to hide.

There was the slightest whisper of sound. Martin dove to his left and brought his shotgun to bear. He saw the shadow land just as he hit his head and the night vision flipped up. He fired blindly and was rewarded with the screech the things made when they were hurt. He took a second to flip his night vision down and looked around and up. There was a spread-eagled shape almost on top of him. He lifted his gun to block it, and the vampire slammed into it. The weight forced him to the ground. The fangs were inches from his face when his finger pulled the trigger. The vampire exploded.

Martin spat dust and vampire bits from his mouth and looked around again. He was alone in the cave. He took a moment to thoroughly check, but there was no other place for a vampire to hide. He spat again, then took a long drink from his canteen. He still tasted blood in his mouth. He washed his mouth out and realized that he'd bit his tongue when he fell.

The tunnel was just as creepy on the way back. There was a bag hanging in the center of the big hole, maybe ten feet up. As soon as he cleared the tunnel he checked in.

"Martin here," he said. "There was one in a cave at the end of the tunnel. There was no exit. That's three down."

"There's some food and drink in the bag along with your extra guns." Reba said. "Take a minute to eat and drink before you do the last tunnel."

Martin didn't feel very hungry, but he forced himself to eat the sandwiches and empty the water bottle. He loaded up with more magazines, it was time to search out the last of these creatures and blow them full of holes.

He carried the regular shotgun, but had the other one loaded and ready. The machine pistol was strapped to his right leg. Magazines were strapped to his left. He had four left.

Once again the tunnel was a cleft in the rock. This one felt roomier. A glance upward showed that the ceiling was rising. Martin kept the shotgun pointed upward as he walked along the tunnel. Even with all his caution, the next attack took him by surprise. It was only the upward pointing shotgun that saved him. The vampire landed on the end of the shotgun. The blow twisted it enough that it fired. This time Martin didn't take much more than the time to spit the vile taste of vampire away from his mouth.

His finger was on fire. It was twisted at a strange angle. He swore and snapped it back into position. It still hurt, but he thought it would fire a gun. He picked up the shotgun and kept going.

He heard a rustle before the next attack. There were two of them, but he emptied the shotgun at one of them, then used the machine pistol on the other one. Before he had time to celebrate he heard more rustling. He reloaded the machine pistol and dropped the shotgun just as hundreds of rats swarmed the tunnel. Something in the way they moved made him think that they were controlled by a vampire. He used the machine pistol to spray them, reloaded and kept shooting. In less than ten seconds he'd used up all his ammo on the rats and reduced the vermin to smoking bits. He dropped his shotgun and machine pistol and readied the tommy shotgun.

He walked through the carnage and kept hunting. His nose was adjusting to the funk of death in the air. Martin thought he smelled pine trees. If he did then he needed to get the last four vampires before sunset. He had no idea how long he'd been down here. When he looked at his watch it had been smashed. Martin dropped it on the floor.

The air was definitely changing. Martin picked up his step. The tunnel widened, and the ceiling stretched up. He could see a faint grey light high above him.

Three vampires burst from the loose dirt in the floor as the fourth dropped from a ledge above him. Martin fired the tommy shotgun for the first time and blew a hole through one of the three on the floor. He shifted to the side to avoid the falling attacker and rolled under the attack of the faster of the two remaining on the floor. He flicked the switch to full auto and took aim at the vampires. He was never going to get a better chance.

The gun hammered at him for three second before it jammed. But those three seconds had turned two of the remaining vampires to dust. He didn't even bother spitting as he ran into the tunnel after the last vampire. He dropped gear as he ran. Anything to make himself faster. The only thing he kept was the knife that was in a sheath in the small of his back.

As he careened through the tunnel in pursuit of his prey, Martin noticed the luminescence of the slime. It was enough for him to follow the tunnel. He only had minutes to catch the last vampire before sunset would allow it to escape. He burst into the large hole and was almost blinded by the last light of the day. He saw the vampire climbing the wall where it was in the shade. He climbed after it.

The first shot blew dirt from the wall near his right hand. Martin jumped to the right, hoping that Reba was adjusting left. He didn't know why she was shooting at him. He shouted up to her, but another shot was proof that she didn't hear him. He had to zig zag up the wall to catch the vampire. He caught up as it reached the lower dead end tunnel. He jumped on the vampire just as a shot burned through his left shoulder. The vampire ran into the dark, and he followed.

There was no luminescence here, just the faint reflected light from the dying day. The vampire jumped on him. Martin twisted to throw the vampire against the wall. Bullets continued to burst against the wall. The vampire jumped at him again, but Martin had the knife in his hand. The vampire ducked and snatched at the knife, ripping it from his hand.

Martin snarled with rage, and as the vampire lunged at him with the knife raised, Martin caught its knife hand with his left hand. His shoulder screamed in agony, but he only needed a second. He plunged his right hand into the vampire's chest and ripped its heart out.

He heard a scream from above and a fifty caliber bullet blew through the vampire and then through Martin. Still holding the vampire's heart Martin fell from the mouth of the tunnel and bounced down the side of the hole. Dirt and rocks tumbled after him and buried him alive. The last thing he was conscious of was the taste of blood in his mouth.

Epilogue

Bill lowered a flashlight to the bottom of the hole, but he couldn't see any sign of the vampire that fell into the depths. Nothing was moving down there.

"I nailed the bastard," Reba said through her tears. "Just after it killed Martin." She picked up the big fifty caliber. "Let's get the hell out of here." Bill patted her shoulder awkwardly, then fired up the quad. They rode back to the camp where he bundled her into his car and drove into town with a story that was even crazier than the movie he'd been making.

They started with the Staff Sargent and argued their way up to the Chief's office. It helped that Bill was a high-powered director and his movie had been pouring plenty of cash into the local economy.

"Alright," the Chief said as the sun peeked up over the horizon and stabbed Bill in the eyes. "I'll send a team out to look at the site. Captain Carruthers was handling everything personally. If I find that you're joking with me, there will be serious consequences."

"I haven't slept in more than twenty-four hours. Do you think I could go and sleep somewhere?"

"I don't want you leaving until I know what I'm dealing with."

"Well, lock me in a cell," Bill said, "as long as there is a bed."

The cell stank and the cot was as hard as concrete. Bill was asleep before his head hit the pillow. They woke him up several hours later. The Chief was on the phone with someone from the Center for Disease Control according to Reba, who looked like she hadn't been allowed to sleep at all.

"Someone had to show them the site," she said, "I played them the videos in the trailer and showed them the hole. Now it's someone else's problem." She leaned back against the wall and started snoring gently.

The men in the suits arrived before dark. Bill never caught their names or the agency they worked for. The Chief was happy to hand the entire mess over to someone else.

"This is a matter of national security," the one man in a suit said to Bill. "It was an unfortunate outbreak of some disease. They'll figure out which one later."

"Wouldn't it make more sense to play it as a terrorist attack?" Bill said. "Then the people will be heroes who battled for their country, and there won't be a panic that the disease might have got out of quarantine."

"Will the other movie people buy it?"

"They left after Philson died. If you play it as a mind control drug, his suicide makes sense."

"You're slick," the man looked at Bill suspiciously. "Can I trust you?"

"I'm a director," Bill said, "I know what people want."

"What do you want?"

"I have a bunch of footage that isn't going to be worth much," Bill said and looked the man in the eyes, "unless I turned it into a movie inspired by true events about a terror attack on a movie set."

"Interesting," the man cocked his head as if he were listening to someone else's voice, "how soon could you get it out to theaters?"

"It depends on how much money I have."

***

Martin switched the coverage of the premiere off. He looked at the clock on the wall. It was almost 2 am. The door opened, and a raggedly dressed man walked in.

"Hear you buy blood," the man said, "no tests, no questions."

"That's right," Martin said, "we test the blood later, if we can't use it for the blood bank, we can sell it to researchers. We pay ten dollars a unit."

The man rolled up his sleeve. Martin carefully swabbed the area and inserted the needle. The blood dripped into the collection bag. When it was full, he marked it and paid the man. The company really did sell blood to researchers. They wanted blood with the full range of human disease in it. They made a good deal of money at it.

Enough to pay for around the clock staffing. They were delighted that Martin worked the night shift.

At six, Martin welcomed his day time replacement and picked up his lunch bag. The elevator took him straight to the subway. He waved to the guard as he swiped in. He rode four stops and took another elevator up to the lobby of a mall. A private elevator took him up to his room. He rented it fully furnished, but the only important thing was the refrigerator. He put the blood from his bag into the fridge. As long as the books balanced, no one noticed that he kept some blood from each shift to take home.

Tomorrow was his night off.

Maybe he'd allow himself a treat, and go hunting.

Alex McGilvery

Acknowledgements

The Thing in the Hall started out as a story for contests on Worth1000, though it's seen considerable work since its appearance on that site. *Strange Carnivores* came about as part of a discussion on Wattpad about who would win a fight, vampires or werewolves. I am always something of a rebel and suggested that carnivorous frogs would kick the backside of both of those creatures of the night. It then became necessary to write the story. Lastly *Sparkles and Blood* grew out of a contest on Wattpad to write an old-school vampire story. The temptation to mix the sparkly vampires and the bloody ones was too much to refuse. Wattpad was kind enough to feature the story and it is approaching one hundred thousand reads on that site.

No book comes to print without a lot of work from a lot of people. I need to thank my editors Dean C. Moore and Sarah Brown who worked hard to make these stories look as good as they do. Any mistakes that remain are my responsibility. All the stories have been edited for this release. *Frost and Stone* makes its first appearance anywhere as part of this book. There is a story by that title on Worth1000, but the only thing that remains of that original concept is the names.

Other books by Alex

Wendigo Whispers (Summer 2017)

The Devil Reversed

Generation Gap

The Gods Above

Tales of Light and Dark

Like Mushrooms (poetry and photography)

The Heronmaster

Princess of Boring

By the Book

Sarcasm is My Superpower

Playing on Yggdrasil

The Unenchanted Princess

Alex also has stories in:

Words on the Rocks

Beyond the Wail

Collidor Stream Collection 2016